"I'm over you, Chrissy," Mitch said very softly, putting his hands on her shoulders, tangling his fingers in her dark abundant tresses.

"Then why kiss a woman who's been nothing but trouble?" Christine couldn't resist the urge to taunt him.

"Could be I just think of it as fighting fire with fire."

"So what are you waiting for?" She felt a sudden violent rush of exhilaration in her blood as the weight of his wonderful curvy mouth came down over hers.

It was meant to be a light, mocking kiss that would convey to her she was no longer in his blood. No longer able to drive him to distraction. Only, the kiss changed character....

Dear Reader,

This third story in my KOOMERA CROSSING miniseries
continues the theme of families and bonded lives, the
unique relationships that are formed in isolated outback
life. We all belong to a family, and how we fared in
childhood and adolescence has a powerful effect on
our lives. Some have the great good fortune to be reared
in a loving, stable home where the young are encouraged
to approach life from a positive angle and are always
given a helping hand. Others are always struggling to
win acceptance, to be loved, knowing it's not going to
happen. Eventually, they are forced to make a life far
from their families in order to protect themselves.

Christine is one such heroine who is forced into fleeing her
desert home. In running away she must leave behind the
love of her life, her kindred spirit, Mitch Claydon. He nurses
a bitter hurt and disillusionment while she travels the world
as a glamorous fashion model, but she's unable to forget
the man she's left behind....

The first book in my KOOMERA CROSSING miniseries
was the Harlequin Superromance® novel *Sarah's Baby*.
This was followed by *Runaway Wife* in Harlequin Romance®.
Look for *Outback Surrender*, December 2003, also in
Harlequin Romance®.

Margaret Way

MARGARET WAY
Outback Bridegroom

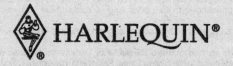

TORONTO • NEW YORK • LONDON
AMSTERDAM • PARIS • SYDNEY • HAMBURG
STOCKHOLM • ATHENS • TOKYO • MILAN • MADRID
PRAGUE • WARSAW • BUDAPEST • AUCKLAND

ISBN: 0-373-03771-6

OUTBACK BRIDEGROOM

First North American Publication 2003.

Visit us at www.eHarlequin.com

Printed in U.S.A.

CHAPTER ONE

IT WAS funny about love, he thought. It never died. Or his particular kind of love didn't: his was unconditional, irreversible. He'd had it once. He'd never found it again. Not since Christine. Always, always, Christine!

If he lived to be one hundred he doubted if he could ever forget his childhood sweetheart, the love of his life, the impossibly beautiful Christine Reardon. Such was their bond right through childhood and their teens—his wretched and—let's face it—unrequited love for her was never going to leave him. He was still spellbound by the very sight of her, though she had used him shamefully. For a man with guts and pride aplenty, that made him feel really bad.

He had learned to love early. Both he and Christine were Outback born and reared. Both were the children of pastoral dynasties—bush aristocracy, as it were. That in itself had forged a powerful connective link. He was Mitchell Claydon, heir to Marjimba Station, she was the granddaughter of the so recently late, unlamented Ruth McQueen, whose wake he and half the Outback were at present attending.

The interment, under a blazingly hot sun, was mercifully over, but the wake, held at the McQueens' historic homestead Wunnamurra, dragged on and on as it befell everyone to pay their respects to such a powerful pioneering family.

For two hours now he had stood suffering blackly—he hoped it didn't show—longing to cool off with a cold beer, not endless cups of tea or the whisky the boys in the library were having. An irreverent thought, maybe. Ruth's funeral was a momentous day in their part of the world—vast Outback Queensland, an endless source of fascination to most of the country who led city lives. Ruth, ex-matriarch of the McQueen dynasty, was not your normal much mourned grandmother. Ruth in her lifetime had had a patent on seriously ruthless behaviour, but she'd had the aura and financial muscle to somehow pull it off.

He'd never liked her. In fact he'd come close to loathing her, so how could he be expected to mourn her passing? Wasn't the reason Christine had run away from him to escape her grandmother's clutches? Or so Chrissy had claimed. One way or the other, Christine's flight had been swift and terrible for a girl who up to that time had declared her endless love for him. The fervour with which she'd said it still rang in his heart like a bell.

"How I love you, Mitch!" That tone should have been kept for worship. Her face had been luminous as a pearl above him, her thick braid undone, silken hair glistening even in the scented darkness of their special place, a pink lily pond few other people came to or even knew. Her beautiful hands had always smelled of boronia, caressing his naked chest, spiralling downwards, in delicate stroking circles that had made his blood run molten, his body shaking with the fine tremors of blind passion.

An inferno of desire! He would have done anything for her. She had power, great power, in the age-old manner of beautiful seductive women. It was this that had mesmerized him. Kept him captive so he never saw all the other girls who tried to win his attention.

Christine. Always Christine.

Her ardent declarations had turned out to be utter lies. She had betrayed him and played him, scorning the love she'd proclaimed so sublime. The grief and the anger Mitch felt had gone so deep they still burned brightly. So why, then, couldn't he forget her? Wash his hands of her? Get on with his life?

It hadn't worked out like that at all. God knows he'd tried. And now he stood in Wunnamurra's very grand drawing room watching the assembled family saying goodbye to the last of the mourners. There was much solicitous air-kissing, diplomatic condolences, though the departed Ruth had been disliked with a passion. Not that Ruth had minded while she was alive. In fact she'd actively encouraged such strong sentiments in those she considered her inferiors, and they included the entire Outback at one time.

Vale, Ruth! Arrogance and snobbery personified.

Kyall was an entirely different story. No one could tarnish Kyall McQueen's image. Kyall had been his friend from earliest childhood, as was Kyall's fiancée, Sarah Dempsey—Sarah Dempsey—head of Koomera Crossing's Bush Hospital.

Ranged beside Kyall and Sarah on the farewelling line were Kyall's mother and father, Enid and Max, a mightily dysfunctional couple if ever there was one, and beside them Kyall's problematic young cousin, Suzanne, dragged home from boarding school. But the ultimate object of Mitch's attention this long, terrible day was the stunning young woman standing protectively beside Suzanne like some exotic long-legged waterbird.

Christine. His only love! Hell, weren't they great days, when love had surged sweet and absolutely irresistible? So irresistible it sometimes seemed to him his emotional life hadn't taken one single step forward. As for Chris? Her life had gone ahead in great leaps and bounds. It was a long hike from awkward adolescent, head ducking, shoulders slouching in an effort to hide her height, to fêted international model who regularly bagged the cover of well-known international magazines.

The moment he'd laid eyes on her that morning she'd been walking with immense style down Wunnamurra's grand divided staircase. That catwalk training had been devastatingly successful, he'd noted cynically.

God, what a knockout! He, despite everything, felt pierced again by love's maddening arrows. The poor schmuck who stared up at her as if she was a goddess favouring earth with a visit. Who could take that much heart-stopping beauty? He'd only stared, feeling his tormented heart banging away so loudly he'd thought it might leap from his chest. Such weakness dishonoured him. From that moment on his pride had made it easier...

"Mitch, how wonderful to see you again!" Her stunning, high-cheekboned face turned on the now famous smile. "It's so good of you and the family to come."

Some moments spin out forever. Memories invaded his mind, one scene opening out after the other. Always he and Chris together—riding, swimming, skinny-dipping in the creeks across Marjimba, exploring the Hill Country, exploring each other's excitable young bodies. God knows how he'd found the gumption to move, but he had.

"Hey, we're family, aren't we, Chrissy?" He'd sauntered up to her, hadn't attempted to hug her, or kiss her cheek. He'd settled for a sardonic handshake. She wouldn't like the "Chrissy", but he'd just wanted to let her know he'd never accept the usual baloney. "Wonderful to see you" rang ludicrously untrue after the way she'd treated him.

That had been twenty minutes before the trip to the family cemetery, where Ruth had been interred with the pomp she certainly didn't deserve. Since then his emotions had threatened by the minute to get seriously out of hand. A big mistake. These days he was very much a man in control. He considered it a by-product of being dumped by the said Christine. He didn't look for love any more. Love was a four-letter word. Now he settled for companionship. Sex. He was tempted, like the next man. And this way there would be no stress, no pain. Sometimes a lot of fun, but that was the end of it. Still, it was lousy when you couldn't fall in love again.

Christine, his heart's desire, was woven warp and woof into the fabric of his life, and it looked as if he'd have to wrestle with that one forever. She'd become so finely polished, like a diamond, he could hardly bear her brilliance. Neither could he look away. Enid's "ugly duckling" had long since turned into a swan. He'd always known she would.

In her adolescence Enid and Ruth had hardly a kind word to say to Chris regarding her coltish, somewhat androgynous look, the insouciant "boy" in jodhpurs and shirts. Of course she'd cultivated the look deliberately, in retaliation, and quietly laughed about it as he kissed and caressed her beautiful, very feminine breasts.

Petite women, Enid and Ruth had privately and very publicly agonized over Chris's height as though it were none of their fault. So Chris was six feet? Tall for a woman, certainly, but they had been so cruel!

Christine in those days had been like a creature of the wild trapped in a cage. And she had fled her unhappy home. Anyone who'd had anything to do with Enid and Ruth could understand that. Except she'd fled him when he'd thought they had never been more in love. Hell, he'd been five minutes away from marrying her.

She was nineteen, he just twenty-one, and stupid enough to think he was God's gift to women. Girls had liked to tell him that. Hard to believe, but true. Not Christine. She'd called him many a nasty name, ranting and raging that she had to find herself before she could deal with him. Marriage. Kids. Had he ever considered, given their combined height—he was six-two—their children might finish up as basketball stars?

What was wrong with that? They'd fought terribly. He'd had every confidence he would win. He knew he'd acted as if he equated her pending defection to committing a serious crime. But it was the pain and the sense of loss that had enraged him. A grief so acute it had resulted in his saying a lot of things that should never have been said.

Hadn't she promised when she turned fourteen that they were going to get married? He'd thought both of them had taken that promise very seriously. Neither of them had wanted anyone else. He realised how stupid all of that was—kids' stuff—except his feelings had never changed. He hadn't even learned to be truly unfaithful. The flesh was weak but the mind remained purely loyal.

Now Ruth McQueen's death had brought Christine home. For how long? A couple of days? A week? Surely she could spare some time off? She loved her father and brother; she tried hard to love her difficult, distant mother; she seemed to have taken charge of Suzanne. She didn't need the money—Christine had a very tidy trust fund—but she did need that sense of self her success had brought her.

Always beautiful to him, she had made big changes. Gone was the slouch, the dip of the head to make herself shorter. How often had he tried to encourage her out of that? She'd always looked great to him no matter what she wore. Easy, casual. Now her clothes were the epitome of cosmopolitan chic. Dressed head to toe in sombre black, she nonetheless resembled an elegant brolga among what was in the main a flock of dull magpie geese.

She had learned patience. She'd stood throughout the ceremony in a contemplative mood. It must have been easy enough to conjure up her never well-intentioned late grandmother of the acid tongue. She'd shown no sign of nervousness or the inattention which had warranted many admonitions in the old days. Occasionally she'd smiled. The smile, now famous, lit up her face, displaying her beautiful teeth. He still had her early toothpaste ad hidden away in a drawer. It was almost in tatters from the countless times he'd looked at it. Once he'd had an impulse to tear it up—ever after grateful he hadn't.

Christine! What a class act.

A kind of rage fuelled him. He who loved this goddess risked losing his head. Just being in the same room with her after years of estrangement put him in a strange mood, where anger and the pain of rejection lay heavily on his heart. He was profoundly conscious time was passing. All his friends were either getting engaged or married. When the hell was he going to surrender? He had to know he wouldn't want for prospective brides.

Christine hadn't married either, though he hadn't the slightest doubt her phone kept ringing off the hook. For years he'd secretly followed her career as revealed by the tabloids. Her name had been linked with several highly eligible bachelors on the international scene, including an up-and-coming American actor who apparently featured in some TV soap five afternoons a week.

Strangely enough, the actor wasn't unlike him. His mother had pointed him out on a magazine cover. The same physical type—tall, blond hair, blue eyes. Was it possible it had struck Christine too in passing? *Say, this guy looks a bit like Mitch. Remember Mitch? Your first lover. He would have fought for you. Slaved for you. Died for you. He would have sold the family farm for you. He would have done all of that. He really loved you.*

In the end she had taken off. Defection. What she had left behind her was poor old Mitch Claydon with a broken heart.

Across the room his mother gave him a wave, indicating they were about to fly home. His expression, unconsciously taut, softened. He loved his mother. She was a good woman with a brightness about her. These days he did all the piloting. His dad preferred to go along as a passenger.

He and Christine had barely exchanged a word. He'd had more to say to her young cousin Suzanne, who had to be all of sixteen. In the old days he and Christine had thrown their arms around each other, kissing, hugging, even when they'd seen one another the night before. They hadn't been able to get enough of each other. Then. Loving to spend all their free time together. They'd even had their own fairy tale going. He was to rescue her from the clutches of her wicked grandmother…

Pure wishful thinking! Now so much time had passed. Time and change and pain. Christine was back. How in the world was he going to deal with it?

Christine hoped he wasn't aware of it, but she'd been watching him endlessly, full of aches and regrets, memories she'd never been able to put out of her mind. Years of separation might have begun yesterday. Mitch still had the same magnetic drawing power that had captured her heart in the first place.

He was hard to miss. Mitch Claydon was a legitimately dashing guy. Golden-boy handsome, compellingly heterosexual. Almost rare in her world, where good-looking male models abounded, scarcely a one of them straight. Mitch would never enter her kind of world. Mitch had grown up accomplishing things, with a wonderfully pleasing and sunny nature. Mitch was a bred-in-the-bone cattleman, from a family with a rich pastoral tradition, a family very much like her own. Except the Claydons didn't fall into the dysfunctional category. Mitch's parents were and remained loving partners, committed to their family, openly demonstrative.

After their big break-up, somewhere along the line Mitch had developed an air of total inaccessibility. His gaze told her very plainly, *Look, I might have loved you once, but I'll never let you in again.* Even the way he'd greeted her earlier in the day had told the same story. A white smile on his golden-skinned face, eyes sea-blue, sometimes turquoise, depending on his mood, always brilliantly twinkling as if there were stars at their centre, that thick soft golden pelt a woman would die for brushing his collar, but behind the smooth façade a great big sign that said: *Back Off!*

It made her incredibly unhappy, but she thought she was covering it well. Her model training was the perfect camouflage. She could provide expressions on demand.

In her experience men like Mitch were outside the ordinary. They stood out in life, not simply because of their looks, which were remarkable enough, but because of their aura of self-confidence. In some it almost bordered on arrogance, except it was the arrogance of achievement, of skills beyond the norm. The McQueens and the Claydons had established pastoral empires. Men like Mitch and her brother Kyall made it work. Without them, and men like them, their considerable enterprises would go under, their properties be dispersed.

It had happened with her own father's family, the Reardons. Such was the McQueen name, and her grandmother's power, her brother Kyall had actually been christened Kyall Reardon-McQueen, to be universally known as Kyall McQueen by the time he was three years old. And nothing to be done about it! Whereas she, the girl, and therefore not in the running for the top job, was Christine Reardon. Extraordinarily enough, even her father under-

stood Kyall was a McQueen, with all that entailed. She had
never heard him snipe about it.

She glanced over at her parents. They were deep in conversation with the Claydons. Her heart quivered as she
stared at her father. He had never had an easy time of it.
Not with her domineering mother and grandmother. Things
had never been good at Wunnamurra, where disharmony
prevailed. She often wondered how her parents had come
together in the first place, their personalities were so different. Eventually she and Kyall had decided it was more
a marriage of suitable families than a love match.

Her grandmother, Ruth, had made everyone uneasy. She
hadn't attempted to disguise her contempt for her granddaughter's "tawdry career"—and tawdry did enter into it
at some points. That couldn't be denied. Alcohol, drugs,
sexual predators—even among the very people there to protect you. Some of her friends in the business found it a
battlefield, but she'd always been able to keep her feet
firmly planted on the ground. All that mattered was to love
and be loved in return. For all her successes she had never
achieved that.

Not since Mitch, who had clearly put her behind him.

Love was a beautiful plant. If it wasn't nurtured it would
eventually wither and die. She hadn't arrived at that point.
It seemed Mitch had. She didn't blame him.

A part of her had never left her Outback home, just as
a part of her had always feared to return. Too much stress
she didn't want to handle. Although she thought she had
changed a good deal—certainly she had become self-
reliant—she knew it mightn't take long before the old sense
of worthlessness began to pervade her. Such was her
mother's and, to a much greater extent, her grandmother's
corrosive effect on her. Now her grandmother had been

removed from the scene. Laid to rest. Or she was off some place else, terrorizing people.

A warm cheerful voice spoke as a hand touched her shoulder. "Christine, we're off! It's so lovely to see you again, dear." In a flurry of genuine affection Mitch's mother, Julanne, a handsome blonde woman with beautiful skin, embraced her. "Please don't run away too soon. It's so wonderful to have you home. I'd love it if you could visit us for a few days. There's so much I want to talk to you about. Please say you'll spare us a little time?"

Out of the corner of her eye Christine saw Mitch approaching with his familiar dashing, athletic grace. "I don't know if Mitch would like that, Mrs Claydon." Her tone was a mix of rueful and very wary. She'd seen the masked hostility spilling out of Mitch's beautiful light-filled eyes.

"You don't have to worry about Mitch," Julanne whispered back, following Christine's glance. "Deep down you two could never be anything else but friends. I always understood why you went away, my dear."

"I had to, Mrs Claydon. The simple, unvarnished truth."

"I know that." Julanne Claydon appeared to consider her next words with great care. "But things will be easier now, with your grandmother gone. She was a truly extraordinary woman, but she could cause great tension."

Christine nodded. "She wanted perfection—or her kind of perfection. Sadly for me, I couldn't deliver. Mum and Gran saw eye to eye on one point. They wanted a doll they could dress up."

"And what they got was an absolutely beautiful young woman. Inside and out."

"Thanks for that, Mrs Claydon." Christine smiled at this very kind, supportive woman who had always been her friend.

"Julanne, please, love. No need to call me Mrs Claydon any more. I watched you grow up."

"And up!" Christine the supermodel raised her eyes heavenward, such was the drubbing she'd received about her height.

"It's because of your height and those lovely long limbs you've become so famous, dear," Julanne pointed out. "You must know that."

"I do." On an impulse Christine kissed the older woman's cheek. "I've never forgotten your kindnesses to me."

"You were very easy to be kind to, Christine," Julanne responded, remembering how Christine had been virtually ignored while all the love and attention was focused on her brother Kyall. "So you'll come? I'm starved for some colour and excitement. Think of all the stories you can tell me."

"Some stranger than fiction," Christine only half joked. "Well, then, it's a date—and thank you for always being so nice to me. Give me a little time to sort out an agenda and I'll let you know."

"Mitch can come for you," Julanne suggested, never having given away her dream that some day her son and Christine Reardon would patch up their differences and make a match of it. After all, for many long years they'd been a perfect circle of four. Mitch and Christine. Kyall and Sarah.

"Mitch can do what?" There was challenge, maybe an edge of animosity beneath the silken enquiry.

She steeled herself to turn around, tension showing in every line of her body. Earlier in the day she had known moments of pure exultation when they'd first come face to face. They might never have been parted; her attraction had been running at full throttle and she'd found herself remembering all the wonderful times, the bad times, full of shouting and tears. Now, heart thumping, she looked steadily into the compelling eyes that had haunted her. ''Your mother will tell you, Mitch. I fear I don't dare.'' He looked absolutely marvellous to her, even with his bronze brows drawn together.

''That's not the Christine I knew. She wasn't scared to say anything.''

It was out in the open. Cold war.

Julanne felt it like a stiff breeze. She took her son's arm in her cajoling fashion. ''Mitch, darling, I've asked—no, begged—Christine to visit us while she's home. There's so much for us all to catch up on.''

''That'd be great,'' Mitch said in a honeyed drawl. ''I suppose.''

''You don't sound too sure?''

He pretended to think a moment. ''Of course we'd love to have you, Chrissy. It's been so very long. But we'll take no notice of that. I suppose you're keen to get back to the Big Apple. And that guy—what's his name?'' He made his tone admiring.

''I don't have a guy,'' Christine retorted with determined cheerfulness, recognising the taunt. How could she when the same old feelings for Mitch were smashing through her? Wave after wave of white-water thrills, going deeper and deeper into her body, leaving her feeling shaky and so vulnerable. Mitch had always been good for that. Wonderful, glorious thrills.

Now he smiled affectionately at his mother. ''Let's refresh your memory. What's his name, Mum? You showed me his picture in some magazine.''

''Oh, sure. I know. Ben Savage,'' Christine cut in, before Julanne could answer. ''I don't see Ben any more.''

"That's sad. What happened?" He faced her, neatly trapping her gaze.

"None of your business, Mitch."

He gave her a slow smile, dangerous, taunting. "Except there was something familiar about the guy…"

"The first thing that drew me to him was his resemblance to you."

"Hell, I would have thought it was enough to condemn him!" The tension between them was mounting so quickly it was monstrous, nearly physical, startling them all.

"Ah, Mitch." Christine gently moaned, she felt so bad. "Ben's very nice. Just like the character he plays. Warm, caring, comforting."

His eyes rested compulsively on the small velvety beauty spot high up on her right cheekbone. He'd always loved it. Nothing had changed, however much he wanted it. His heart, for all its loneliness and isolation hadn't frozen over. "Then why the break-up?" he asked.

"When I figure it out you'll be the first to know."

"I'd appreciate that, Chrissy."

"Listen, children," Julanne intervened hurriedly, flustered by the frozen sparks, "be nice to each other. You're friends, not enemies. I'll leave you to say goodbye. Please be in touch, Christine."

"I'll call you," Christine promised, very nervous now that Julanne had moved away.

Mitch laughed sardonically in his throat. "Some day Mum's going to wake up to the fact we're not kids any more. No longer girlfriend and boyfriend heading towards the altar."

"Mothers do that all the time. Some mothers," she added, reflecting for a minute on her own. "What about you, Mitch? How have you managed to stay a bachelor?"

"I get offers all the time," he said flippantly.

"Have you any idea why?"

Even her voice, with its acquired layer of American accent, glittered. Just like the old days whenever he'd rattled her. *"Touché!"* He gave a short laugh. "I want you to know I'll reject any offer of yours."

"You sound like you're expecting me to make one."

"Believe me, I'm considered eligible and you're not getting any younger. Must be about time to have thoughts of settling down, Chrissy. You can't stay a top model permanently. I make it you'll be thirty in two years' time."

"Did you get my card for *your* thirtieth?" She'd been in London at the time, for an important shoot.

"No, I didn't."

"Stupid me. I must have forgotten to send it."

"Chrissy, darling, that's bloody obvious. Hard to believe we were once best friends. I'd say lovers, only I'd bite off my tongue."

"I haven't forgotten, Mitch," she said quietly, her blue eyes finding his.

"Please!" His voice had a contemptuous lilt. "Spare me the long poignant look. I'm Mitch, remember? The poor fool who used to love you? For years I couldn't seem to stop, but eventually the heart sickens." He could have kicked himself; it had come out way too bitterly. "I was the one left broken up, Chrissy. I figure you got what you always wanted. To be someone."

She looked away from his taut, exciting face. The old Mitch had been so sweet, so carefree. "If you feel this bad I shouldn't visit."

He responded with a decided edge in his voice. "Listen, Chris, we might hate each other, but Mum loves you, and my mother is very dear to me. If she wants you to visit, I want you to visit. I swear I'll be on my best behaviour, no matter how great the effort."

''That might present a few problems.'' Even so she knew nothing would stop her.

''A dilemma.'' His agreement came swiftly.

''And to think I brought you home a present.'' She had searched for something to please him.

''I swear I won't open it.''

''Then you can burn the damned thing. Really, Mitch, I don't mind.''

''Such a world of sorrow in a dead love!'' he lamented. ''Some heroine you were! Remember, I was your knight? I was going to save you from the fire-breathing dragon. Or dragoness. Your grandmother. Well, now she's gone.''

''Poor Gran,'' Christine said. ''No one mourns her.''

''That would be kind of silly, wouldn't it? She hurt so many people.''

''Of course she did.'' Even now Mitch didn't know the whole truth.

''Let's forget Ruth, even if it is her wake. How long are you staying?''

''I've got nothing to hurry back to.'' She wasn't about to tell him her career had palled. Just how many designer outfits could she continue to get in and out of? How many more photographic shoots could she bear? Freezing in summer clothes in the middle of winter! That might get a cruel laugh. The old Mitch had never been cruel.

He just looked at her. ''What does that mean?''

''It seems to me I've worked long and hard enough to deserve a holiday.'' She did her best to sound casual.

''Aren't you worried they might find a fresh face, in the meantime, a great body to match it?''

''No.'' She answered with truth. ''To become a top model wasn't the reason I ran off.''

His expression was downright scornful. ''Chrissy, you amaze me! I distinctly remember your saying that was all you were good for, and it was so patently untrue. It wasn't just Kyall who shone at school. You did too. Though I know apart from Kyall and your father the rest of your family took no damned notice. You could have been anything you wanted to be. I'd have waited.''

''No, you wouldn't!''

That burst from her, and she couldn't call the fiery taunt back. It was her first show of anger, the first indication he was getting to her. By sheer force of will she pulled back.

''You had to have what you wanted,'' she said bleakly. ''It just so happened you wanted me all gift-wrapped and home-delivered. But I wasn't ready. I couldn't breathe. Not in my own home. Not anywhere. I was too stressed out, mentally and emotionally. You didn't really understand. How could you? You come from a happy, loving family, full of respect and mutual admiration. You were born self-confident, sure of your place in the world. I was pretty well abandoned, just like poor Suzanne. I've got to do something for her.''

''Thank God she's too short to move into the modelling world,'' he retorted brutally, out of a kind of bewilderment and grief.

''You didn't have to say that.''

'No, I didn't. I'm sorry. Anyway, you saved me from having a real guilt trip about not being supportive enough.''

''We were too young to get married, Mitch.'' She turned her palms up helplessly, her beautiful face imploring.

''I wish my memory of it was that good.'' Bitterly he concentrated on her hands, not the powerful seduction of her face. That too was a mistake. He remembered how those long fingers had felt on his skin, the way she'd used them to excite him. ''Like a fool, I thought you were as madly in love with me as I was with you. You could have warned me. In those days I must have been a total dolt.''

She laughed aloud. Not out of humour. "You may not want to hear this, but, yes, you were. It was important for me to find myself. I was so immature, dependent. I couldn't rush into marriage."

"Very wise," he returned acidly. "Maybe you'd be kind enough to tell me—have you found yourself now?"

"Have you?" They were two beats away from a first-class public row.

"I don't know what I needed to find," he answered, his voice cool and cutting. "I thought I had you. We could have taken it slowly if that was what you wanted."

"Slowly? We were mad for each other. We made love all the time. You couldn't wait to have me. We were bits of kids and you were pushing for marriage."

"Weren't you?" he asked, half savagely. "How many times did you tell me that? You couldn't stand not being with me. You were sad and angry all the time we were apart. Was that all lies."

"Not lies," she muttered with quiet desperation. "I was afraid, Mitch. I had problems. I couldn't face them at home. I had to get away. I had to be separate from my mother and grandmother. Even from you. Like I said, I had to find myself."

"I understand a lot, Chrissy. I was there. But you had my proposal of marriage. My first and my only. I would have done anything for you. Protected you. Loved you. But you said no. That was your decision. I suppose I should say thank you for it now, but at the time it wasn't good for a guy's ego."

"Not one as big as yours, Mitch Claydon—Golden Boy." She gave him the full battery of her hostile sapphire eyes.

"What you see is what you get." To her utter surprise he laughed. He knew of old how she used her eyes as weapons. "Now, a few people are looking our way. I don't think this is the day for us to show animosity towards one another, is it, Chrissy? I'm a man who enjoys a peaceful life."

"Pity you can't get it." She averted her head to acknowledge a departing mourner.

"Not with you around, old chum!"

"Is that what we were?" Her reaction was to stare back in open challenge. "Chums? Even when we were best friends we used to fight."

"And forget it the next minute. We couldn't stand to fall out."

"I feel pretty much the same now," she said. Mitch, with his golden mop of hair and star-spangled eyes. He had been such a handsome, engaging boy, full of vitality and high spirits. He wasn't that Mitch any more. "I haven't come back to upset you, Mitch."

"Are you sure?" His voice seared.

"I'm sure." Little ripples of excitement chased themselves down her spine, sliding over bone and muscle, reaching her legs. Excitement had always been part of their relationship.

"That's good, because as it turns out you can't," he informed her. "Losing you taught me a lot, Chrissy. It wasn't a pleasant episode in my life but it was a valuable lesson all the same. I'm damned if I'll ever pay homage to you again."

"When did I ever ask for it?"

"Every goddamn time you were in my arms." Mindful of where they were, he let his voice remain low, but it was freighted with anger.

"I loved you, Mitch." She turned her face up to his, her beautiful skin a perfect foil for the black sombreness of her outfit.

"In a pig's eye you did," he retorted crudely, looking at her with open disgust.

She knew she turned pale. "How can I possibly visit Marjimba with you there?"

"Hell, Chrissy, I'll make sure we're not alone together." He so desperately wanted to grab her, carry her off. He shoved his hands in his pockets. "Today we're just clarifying the situation. Don't ever give me the 'I loved you' bit. I fell for it once. I won't again. Just telling you makes me feel better. I'll be sociable when you visit. There's no end to the things I'll do for my mother. She always did have a soft spot for you, so please do accept her invitation."

"In that case I wouldn't miss it for the world!" She drew a deep, steadying breath, feeling his condemnation like a spear in the heart. "I can see hugs and kisses are clearly out of the question, so take my hand," she said with determined civility.

For an instant it seemed he would refuse. "People are watching, Mitch. You're one of the good old boys, remember?"

He hesitated again, taut and afraid, before he wrapped his strong golden-brown fingers around hers.

Electricity crackled, spat, burned. They might have been alone in a room where everyone else had vanished in a puff of smoke.

A great deep thrust of primitive desire slammed into his body. She had known that was going to happen. He broke contact immediately, his callused hands feeling seared. Had he really thought anything could change? He couldn't control this. He'd wanted her then. He wanted her now. Beyond that ever more aching want.

Hell, what a sorry plight!

CHAPTER TWO

CHRISTINE'S family were at dinner after what had been, all in all, an extraordinarily upsetting day. It was strange to see her mother take pride of place in her grandmother's huge carver chair at the head of the long antique table. Both of them small women, somehow her grandmother had dominated the large space, whereas her mother looked as if her feet dangled clear off the ground.

For once her father occupied the elaborately carved mahogany carver at the other end, having been asked by Kyall to do so. "Take your rightful place, Dad," Kyall urged as they all went to sit down in the places Ruth McQueen had allotted them in her lifetime. "You're head of the family. Everything about the way Gran treated you was terrible."

His mother, ever one to hide her head in the sand, gasped aloud. "Kyall, how can you possibly say that?"

"Because it's true, Mum," he responded bluntly. "I'm sorry if that word isn't in your dictionary."

"Really, Kyall, it doesn't matter," Max intervened.

"It does matter, Dad." At the end of this long strange day, Kyall's normally controlled temper was at flashpoint. "I think we can stop all this stupid business of Kyall McQueen as well. I'm your son, Dad. I love you. I'm a Reardon."

"Bravo!" Christine dared to put her hands together. "Then you can acknowledge I'm your sister as well."

"Don't be silly, Chris."

"Don't take it personally." She smiled at him. "You had nothing to do with it. It was Gran and Mum."

25

Enid looked angrily towards her daughter. "Excuse me, Christine, but your father and I agreed Kyall would be christened Kyall Reardon-McQueen. Didn't we, dear?" Enid appealed to her husband as a good solid mate should.

"We did." Max looked back down the table at her. "We didn't plan on the Reardon being dropped, though, did we?" he pointed out gently.

"It was the town." Enid picked up her wine glass. "The double-barrelled name was too much of a mouthful."

"And God forbid the town should have dropped the McQueen." Christine rolled her eyes at her brother. "After all, the McQueens own it."

"Why is it that you always start something, Christine?" Enid asked, her cheeks flushed a dull red. "You're only just home and you're—"

"Leave her alone, Enid," Max said, his handsome face composed into firm lines.

Enid's hand, mid-way to her wine glass again, froze. "Sometimes, Max, you act like I'm not Christine's mother," she complained. "I've spent the last twenty-eight years of my life being anxious about her."

"I wonder why, Mum?" Kyall asked bleakly. "Chris has made a big success of herself, yet you and Gran spent your time trying to convince her she was an oddity, all long arms and legs. Don't you know how cruel the two of you were to her?"

"Please, Kyall," implored Christine, who had inherited much of her father's peacemaker manner. "Let it drop. We're all upset."

"I certainly am," Enid huffed, secure in the mistaken belief she had taken her responsibilities as a mother seriously. "My mother has only just been buried. Did any of you notice?"

"I don't know that burying Gran is enough for me,"

Kyall said with black humour. "It's not as though she can
stop off at the pearly gates. But I'm sure she'll work out a
deal at the dark end of town."

"Kyall!" Enid's face was shocked. "That's dreadful!"

"Maybe, but I don't like her chances of going to
heaven."

"If there is such a place," Enid responded tartly. "It
seems to me we make our heaven and hell here."

Kyall and Max went off to the library. Suzanne made a
quick escape to her room. And Enid signalled by an im-
perious gesture of her right forefinger that she wished to
speak to her only daughter.

"What do you make of Suzanne?" she asked in a worried tone of voice when they were seated in Enid's spacious
study, door shut.

"Make of her? Gosh, Mum, why throw that at me?
Suzanne's family. I mean, is that any way to put it?"

"You've got a better way?" Enid asked, looking as if
she very much wanted to hear it.

"Keep that tone up, Mum, and I'm ready to leave,"
Christine promised wryly, thinking that whenever she came
into contact with her mother there was confrontation.

"Good grief, Christine, I don't want any arguments."
Enid looked genuinely victimized. "I never know how to
talk to you; you're so different."

"That's why I stay away." Christine stared around the
room, cluttered with trophies and photographs of her
brother. She and Kyall were so alike, but being a female
was her stumbling block. It was splendid to be a male of
six foot plus. Problematic in a female. For years she'd been
made so self-conscious it had been all she could do to cross
a room without stumbling over the furniture.

"I understood you stayed away because of your grandmother.'' Enid pressed back in her comfortable armchair. ''God knows, she gave us all hell—but things are different now. I want to do the best I possibly can for you, and for Suzanne. She is, after all, Stewie's child. I loved my brother. We were such lonely, largely ignored children.''

Christine, never the daughter *her* mother had wanted, laughed. ''Join the group. Let's face it, Mum, beside Kyall I wasn't worth paying any attention to. Kyall was everything. It should have made him unbearable, but it didn't turn out that way. He's a good man. He deserves his Sarah. As for me, I was judged exclusively on my looks. I wasn't the lovely little doll you wanted.''

''You had no interest in clothes.'' Her mother made the charge as though it were important. ''Except boys' shirts and jodhpurs. I was worried you might have 'problems'. Why, after all this time, have you decided to tackle me about it?''

''Maybe I'm trying to work off my own hurt and angry feelings, Mum. You gave me a terrible image of myself. It took me years before I could believe what everyone else was telling me. I'm among the best in the business.''

''My dear Christine, you look fine. Is that what you want to hear? Because it's perfectly true. At thirteen, fourteen and the rest that was far from the case. You slumped badly. I was very worried about your height and your posture. I didn't know when you were going to stop growing. That's the first thing people notice when they meet you for the first time. Your height. And you will wear ludicrously high heels.''

''I've come to terms with my height, Mum. Why can't you? It's so trivial, anyway. I hope there's a whole lot more to me than my looks. They don't last forever.''

''True.'' Enid smoothed her thick, glossy dark hair, which she persisted in wearing too short. ''I try to do the best I can. I was never a beauty, like Mother, but I do look good when I dress up. At any rate I won your father's heart.''

"Oh, Mum…'' Christine, who loved her father dearly and was aware of his unhappiness, almost moaned. "Isn't it time for you to make it up to Dad? He's never had an easy time, with Gran running everyone's life. Why don't you two go on a world trip? Have a second honeymoon? You've heard of a honeymoon, haven't you?''

"Is there something you're trying to tell me, Christine?'' Enid demanded indignantly. A few odd remarks had come to her ears of late, but she hadn't paid much attention. Her marriage vows were set in stone as far as Enid was concerned.

Christine tried a gentle warning. "There's just so much you can do to make things better. A lot depends on how you act from now on.''

"Are you trying to tell me your father isn't happy?'' Enid enunciated, very clearly. "That he might leave me? That isn't his style,'' she scoffed.

"You have to give him that.'' Christine sighed. "But there's no way you can guarantee the future. All I'm saying is, this is yours and Dad's chance at a new life. How is Kyall's marriage going to affect you? Sarah will be mistress of Wunnamurra. You were never very kind to Sarah either. She had to live with that for years. All the snobbery!''

"Sarah has forgiven me.'' Enid stirred restlessly, wanting to bury her part in Sarah's traumas. "And Kyall will still need us to help run the station. Your father and I are very involved in every aspect of the operation.''

"Kyall could easily employ staff if you wanted to do something else,'' Christine suggested.

"Naturally we want to stay here. This is my home,

Christine.'' Enid adopted a fervent tone. ''I was born here. I don't think I could bear to leave it.''

''How does Dad feel? How does Kyall feel? And Sarah's viewpoint is very important.''

''We haven't discussed it.'' Enid rose as if to signify that this oppressive, unwieldy conversation was coming to an end. ''And you, Christine? I'm only your mother, but may I ask your plans?''

Christine lifted her dark head. ''Well, I can't say this is my home, Mum, now, can I? Any more than I can see it as poor little Suzy's home. You're not about to let go, are you?''

So unexpectedly challenged, Enid looked down at her daughter with a mixture of astonishment and disapproval. ''Christine, you're meddling in matters that don't concern you. You know as well as I do Sarah is head of the hospital. That will take up all her time.''

''You don't really believe that, do you? Things change.''

''I don't intend to discuss it with you. You've never involved yourself with the running of Wunnamurra. You left the first moment you could, and I very much doubt if, for all your travels and the glamorous people you've mixed with, you've met anyone who could measure up to Mitchell Claydon. You were very foolish there, Christine. Very headstrong. You actually had Mitchell in the palm of your hand—the entire Claydon family was on side. Even mother approved the match—such a relief—but you flung it all away. For what?''

''The word's freedom, Mum,'' Christine said quietly. ''Until you begin to take a long, hard look at yourself you'll never understand that. Or me.''

''And I've got something to tell you, dear,'' Enid retorted acerbically, well used to having the last word. ''There's a very good chance Mitchell will never forgive you.''

Christine laughed wryly. "Whenever I need comfort, Mum, I come to you. Actually, Julanne has asked me over for a visit."

"When was this?" Enid's dark eyes fired with interest.

"Today."

"Then you'll have to go," Enid said, feeling a wave of maternal hope. Her daughter simply had no idea how she worried about her future. "Mitchell may not have lost all feeling for you after all. Though he's got plenty of girls after him. That silly little Amanda Logan, for one. Throwing herself at him the last time I saw them together. Can't say I blame her. Mitchell is quite a catch. My advice to you is to try and get yourself together. Decide what you want out of life. This may be your very last chance."

Though Christine hated to agree with her mother, it seemed all at once that it was.

Kyall stopped her in the entrance hall, where masses of long-stemmed scarlet roses sat on the circular rosewood library table. Their perfume was a real force.

"Fancy an early-morning ride?" Kyall's smile was full of sweetness and affection.

"What time do I need to get up?" she joked.

"Six okay for you, or are you played out?"

"It's not as though I cried buckets at the funeral." She made a sad face.

"No." His own expression grew bleak.

"And what's the big secret you've all been keeping from me?" She looked steadily into his eyes. "I know there is one. There's more to be told than the miracle of finding your beautiful daughter, Kyall."

"Of course there is, but I won't lay it on you now."

"My God, that bad? Gran probably had a hand in it."

Kyall shook his head quickly, as if he couldn't bear to discuss it then. "I can't wait for you to meet Fiona."

She touched her brother's cheek very gently. "I'm counting the days until I do. My niece. I couldn't be more thrilled for you and Sarah, Kyall. For our family."

"You'll love her, Chris," Kyall promised. "And she'll love you. She's the very image of Sarah, just as we told you."

"And when am I to hear the whole story?"

"Tomorrow," Kyall promised. "We'll ride out around six. Have breakfast together when we come back." He took his sister's face in his hands, dropping a kiss on her forehead. "It's wonderful to have you back, Chris. I've hated the way you moved out of our lives. I've missed you so much. I've missed saying your name."

"I've missed you too, Kyall." Her answering smile was misty.

"We've both had a hard time." He dropped his hands slowly. "It only takes one person in a family to inflict emotional wounds. That one person in ours was Gran. Her power and influence had a devastating effect on us all. Anyway…" He sighed heavily. "Now she's gone we can work all our problems through. What I'd really like to know is how did you go with Mitch? I couldn't help noticing that you were very engrossed in each other."

Christine gave a short unhappy laugh. "Mitch is never going to forgive me."

He gave her a sympathetic look. "I can understand more than most how he feels. You were always together, then you went away. Though I realize you had to make that decision."

"Tell that to Mitch," she said dismally.

"Do you think I haven't? Mitch is my best friend. We've talked a lot about it, but when you're in so much emotional pain it's difficult to achieve objectivity. Everything seemed plain sailing for poor old Mitch. The two of you were going to get married eventually. You were born for each other. Born to live your lives together. You were so much in love.''

"As close as you and Sarah.''

"Both of you left and both of us kind of died,'' Kyall responded with deep, remembered feeling.

"You had relationships.''

"Neither of us would deny it. We're human. But Sarah is and always will be the love of my life.''

"I haven't found anyone to replace Mitch either,'' she confessed.

"You must have had lots of guys wanting a relationship?'' Kyall considered, looking at his beautiful sister.

"I can't commit.'' She made a slight frustrated sound. "Deep down I can't forget Mitch any more than you could forget Sarah. We're alike in that way, the two of us. Single-minded.''

"It can make things very hard at times.'' Kyall pondered. He stared down at his sister, deciding with pride she was stunning. The eyes, the mouth, the skin, the beautiful bone structure revealed by the way she had scraped her long dark mane back into a thick braid, just like she'd used to wear her hair when she was younger. But beyond all that it was a brave face. The face of a young woman who had made her own way in life. "I pray it'll all end well, Chris. I want you to be happy. Mitch too. Both of you are very important to me. It would be wonderful if you could settle back into this life. But you have to contend with the fact Mitch is part of the land like me.''

"Do you think I haven't taken that into account?'' she answered gravely. "The land is your life. Fully and wholly. Perhaps for Mitch even more than for you. You've taken on so many business interests. Suppose I tell you I've missed my Outback home terribly. I'm like the rest of the ex-pats. I have to have Vegemite on my toast and burn a few gum leaves now and again just to recapture the scent of the bush. But you're a man, Kyall. That was and remains the big issue. You've inherited Wunnamurra. I was kept out of it."

"Would you want to run it?" he asked, prepared to extend to her all the sharing she needed.

"No." She laughed and shook her head. "Too much back-breaking work. That's your job, but I reckon I could help. I've been very good with handling my money. Among my peers I'm considered pretty smart."

"You won't get an argument from me." He flashed a smile nearly identical to her own. "Listen, I'd love you to stay, Chris. You could take your rightful place. I have more irons in the fire than even you know. We've diversified a great deal more over the past six or seven years. We've moved into speciality foods and wine. We bought out Beauview Station in the Clare Valley, poured a lot of money into it, secured the services of a great wine maker. You'll have to see it. Now you're home I'd like to fill you in about the family holdings. I could find a nice little place for you on a board or two. I'm certain you've got a head for it. You should really know all about the family assets. You're my sister."

"And I've remained in the dark too long. I'd love to learn all about McQueen Enterprises. I guess that's one reason you're stuck with the name." Christine considered that fact seriously. "To the Outback and the business world you *are* McQueen."

Kyall grimaced. "It's just that I feel guilty about Dad and his feelings."

"You know Dad," she said. "He's accepted it. He

knows the difficulties. He knows you love him. And we're
living proof of him. We have his smile, his height, and his
beautiful blue eyes. It's Mum who doesn't fully appreciate
his worth.''

"Then she might have a problem.'' Kyall put his arm
around his sister's shoulders as they began to walk up the
staircase.

Christine shot him a worried look.

"Dad's seeing someone else, Chris.''

"Oh, God!'' Why wasn't she surprised? "Mum would
die if he left her.''

"Ah, well! Mum's been acting like they're sister and
brother instead of husband and wife. They have separate
suites. She doesn't push him away, and I'm fairly sure she
loves him in her own way, but she doesn't go out of her
way to please him, if you know what I mean. There are
plenty of women in the town who would love to have a
little flutter with Dad. But he's very careful about things
like that. I think, given the situation, he's been extraordinarily faithful, but he hasn't had much of a life. With someone refined and discreet it's another matter.''

"Oh, God!'' Christine repeated on a soft wail. Although
situations like this were commonplace, she hadn't expected
it to strike home. If her mother found out about another
woman could she deal with it?

Christine didn't think so.

Several days later she stood on Wunnamurra's broad verandah, shielding her eyes from the brilliant light of the
sun. She was waiting for Mitch to arrive, to fly her to
Marjimba, having detailed one of the station hands to drive
him from the airstrip to the homestead. She'd timed her
visit to Marjimba to coincide with Kyall's flight to Sydney.

His was a combined exercise—returning Suzanne to her

boarding school and meeting with some new financial people—merchant bankers—McQueen Enterprises was considering dealing with.

There'd been some heart-wrenching moments an hour
earlier when she'd seen Suzanne off. Suzanne had trudged
down the front steps, her vision wavering with tears. The
sight had upset Christine so much she'd found she had to
hold back on her own.

"I hate school." Suzanne had allowed the words to burst
from her lips immediately they were underway in the Jeep.

"Sweetheart, just about everyone hates school."
Christine, at the driving wheel, gave her a sympathetic
glance, "But you haven't got much longer to go. Then it'll
be all over."

"It's been hell trying to hide how I feel. Everyone feels
sorry for you for a while, then they forget. They have no
idea what it's like to lose your parents. You really do love
me, don't you, Chris?" Suzanne sent her cousin such an
appealing look it would have melted stone.

"Hey, of course I love you." Christine reached out her
left hand to squeeze her cousin's delicate shoulder.
"You're my little cousin. I'm only sorry I haven't been
around for you, so we could get to know each other much
better and have some fun. But there's the rest of our lives.
Soon you'll be free to launch yourself on the next exciting
stage of your life. And I'll be there to help."

Suzanne shook her head plaintively. "I wish! But you
fly off overseas all the time."

"I'm considering staying put."

"Are you serious?" Suzanne sounded amazed and delighted.

"Would I lie to you?"

"Actually…no." Suzanne smiled for the first time that

morning. "But what about your modelling? Don't you have to give notice or something?"

"No, sweetie. I don't want you to talk about this—it's a secret for the time being—but I've been giving serious consideration to getting out of the business."

"When you're so hot?"

Christine laughed. "I've had quite a few years on the catwalks and magazine covers. It's not as glamorous as you think."

"But don't you make tons of money?"

Christine turned her head in amusement. "Aren't you the one who said as a family we've all got too much? I don't usually dish out clichés, but money can't buy love and happiness, kiddo. And that's what I want for you."

"I could be happy if you stayed," Suzanne confided. "But what would you do?" she asked with the greatest interest. "You've been so famous. All my girlfriends think you're gorgeous."

"I work at it." Christine smiled. "Genes and a good dose of self-discipline. I've been thinking I might become a businesswoman." She slowed the Jeep as they approached the airstrip. "I have a good head on my shoulders. Kyall wants to teach me the business."

"Oh, that would be great!" Suzanne's soft grey eyes were huge. "You'd stay home in Australia?"

"Those are my thoughts, sweetie. I like the idea of being around for you too. And there's Fiona. I just know you two girls are going to hit if off wonderfully."

Minutes later Suzanne was waving happily from inside the King Air while Kyall took the opportunity to have a few parting words with his sister.

"Well, there's a change. Suzy actually looks happy. What did you say?"

"I promised her I'm going to be around for her. She

needs family badly. She's still in terrible pain from losing her parents."

"Of course she is, poor little mite. But how you're going to be around for her is the burning question, given your career."

"You've offered me options, brother." She smiled into his eyes, relishing the fact he was taller. "At this point I might be ready to start another career."

"Anything that keeps you home suits me. What's more, you have a very good chance of landing our good friend Mitch."

"My now-or-never chance," she said wryly.

"Make the most of it," Kyall urged.

"I will." She held up her face for his kiss.

"You two were meant for each other." Kyall's eyes were serious. "Say hello for me."

"Will do."

Mitch arrived looking like the hero of some Western movie. The one who always got the girl. Irrevocably sunny-natured, with that golden shock of hair, changeable sea-coloured eyes, bold and sparkling against the smooth golden tan, and the irresistible flash of beautiful white teeth.

"Hi!" he called, slamming the door of the open Jeep and sauntering jauntily towards the homestead verandah. He'd promised himself he'd do his level best to be friendly, but he knew he'd have to work hard at it.

"Hi, yourself!" Christine had deliberately posed herself against twin white columns, trying for a touch of humour to break down the expected tensions. After all, they hadn't parted on the best of terms. Indeed, it seemed they would never get back onto their old footing. Such was the price of her defection.

"Chris, you break my heart!" he responded pleasantly,

sweeping off his cream akubra and holding it on cue to his chest. "You're so beautiful, so hot, so sexy! Pity I'm not a photographer." That came out a bit too dryly.

"That's okay. I did dress up a bit, but not in a huge way. Like the outfit?"

"Love it." He ambled up onto the verandah as she broke her pose. "Prairie style, is it?" he asked with mock interest.

"Say, that's knowledgeable." She stared down at herself. She wore jeans with a very feminine cream cotton and lace blouse, and a fancy turquoise buckled belt around her narrow waist. "How did you know?"

He allowed himself a slight laugh, though the sight of her had sharpened his nerves. "Mum has a magazine with you in it looking like some glorious frontier woman, dressed in long suede skirts and high leather boots, with big wide belts and lots of lace and pretty puffed sleeves. Did they know you can ride like the wind?"

"Didn't you notice the one of me on the galloping horse?"

"Hell, I must have missed it." His eyes were sardonic. "I loved the one where you were sitting under a tree strumming a guitar. Nice combination—Victorian blouse, tight sexy jeans and leather boots. But I happen to know you can't play the guitar."

"All right, so *you* can."

"Multi-talented, that's me." He leaned back against a column, still studying her. She was so beautiful. But there was a wall between them he couldn't get around or over. Nevertheless, he was determined to keep to his promise to be sociable. "Remember that stage I went through of trying to yodel?" he asked.

"I remember the falsetto." She turned a smiling face to him, her expression soft and dreamy.

"So why did you keep telling me I could have made it big?"

"As a busker." In fact she'd loved him crooning to her in his smooth melodious voice, her limbs curling up with pleasure. "Mum doesn't want you to leave until you have morning tea."

"I hate morning tea." He mouthed the words.

"Never mind. There are some things a guy's gotta do. Come inside. It's all set up in the garden room. It's abloom at the moment, with some of Mum's spectacular plants."

"This I've got to see." He spoke smoothly. It was a good thing she couldn't hear his pounding heart.

Enid, her fine dark eyes full of bright curiosity, was waiting for them in the double-storeyed light-filled room Ewan McQueen, Christine's grandfather, had built onto the rear of the main house in the early days of his marriage to Ruth.

It was a striking room, distinguished by such an array of exotic plants one had the feeling of being enclosed in a sub-tropical garden. Palms soared, along with golden canes, banana trees, tree ferns, orchids, bromeliads, all kinds of lilium—white, cream, yellow, orange, shocking pink and purple—waxy, highly scented gardenias, colourful pelargoniums, and every variety of philodendron, some with enormous deeply lobed leaves. Everything was grown in pots, and the temperature of the room was controlled by air-conditioning.

As if that weren't enough, Mitch thought wryly, a large Victorian wrought-iron central fountain had been installed, presenting the spectacle and sound of abundant water on the desert fringe. The sparkling emerald green surface was the perfect background for a flotilla of luxuriant creamy-white water lilies.

At home with the McQueens! They sure knew how to live. Whether some of them deserved it was another matter.

His homestead at Marjimba, though big and pleasing, was no possible match for this. Wunnamurra homestead was regarded as one of the finest in the country, and was a showpiece; its rooms were filled with marvellous antiques, the walls aglow with paintings worth a fortune, Chinese porcelains and jade in cabinets, Oriental screens and rugs. You name it, some collector in the family had acquired it. It had been rumoured at one time that Ruth McQueen had an Egyptian mummy secreted away some place. Ruby Hall, Koomera Crossing's resident sticky beak, had blabbed it. He believed that as much as he believed pigs could fly.

"Mitchell, dear!" Enid called to him in a cultured voice that always managed to sound patronising to his ears. "It's so nice of your mother to invite Christine over."

Poor, problematic Christine, he thought, with ongoing resentment towards Christine's autocratic mother. His own home had been more of a shelter and a haven to Christine than this mansion had ever been.

Oblivious to his thoughts, Enid rose from behind a long glass-topped table, extending her hand like royalty.

"How are you, Enid?" He took it gallantly. His mother was big on manners.

She seemed to search his face for something. He wasn't sure what. "Well, I'm doing my best." She sucked in her cheeks. "I miss Mother terribly, of course, but I can't let the rest of the family down. I want this to be a peaceful time for Christine whilst she's here."

"So how long is that to be?" He half turned, caught Christine's eye, his expression as sardonic as hers.

"Just until Mum decides to kick me out." Christine rocked on her boot heels, tucking her hands into the pockets of her jeans.

"Christine, the things you say!" Enid looked exasperated. "You know I hate it when you go away."

Christine smiled broadly. "Gosh, Mum, I've never noticed."

Enid waved a hand at her. "Darling girl, must we air our differences with Mitchell here?"

"He won't stand up for me." She shot Mitch a swift, challenging look.

"You can stand up for yourself," he returned coolly.

"True."

"I had such high hopes for you two," Enid went on to reveal. "To my mind you're perfect husband material, Mitchell."

"Pity Chris didn't think so," he answered carelessly, as though it no longer mattered. "If she had, life would have taken a different turn—wouldn't it, Chrissy?" He glanced at her with light mockery.

"I expect we'd have six or seven kids by now."

"I guess so." He didn't smile, suddenly busy trying to steer out of the rapids.

"You were just too foolish, Christine." Enid shook her head in censure.

"So why isn't anyone desperate to marry you, Mitch?" Christine retaliated, meeting his extraordinary eyes.

"Chrissy, darling, you're way behind the times," he drawled. "Some very nice girls indeed are in the running."

"Annie Oakley out there?"

"There was a time you worked hard at being that, Christine," Enid reminded her. "The arguments we had, trying to get you to put on a dress. Let alone a bit of make-up. Now you're plastered with it."

Christine turned her head towards her mother in mild astonishment. "I wear very little make-up away from the camera, Mum. I'm not wearing much now."

"In your job, I mean." Enid clucked. "You could hardly call it a profession. I'll be so pleased when you're out of it. We all know the dangers. Now…come sit down, Mitchell, dear. I'm sure there's something you'll love here. All freshly baked in your honour. Christine, be a good girl and check if the tea's ready.''

"Sure. I'll nip out to the kitchen right now. You keep Mitch entertained.''

"There are just no words to describe my daughter!'' Enid gave Mitch a half-pained, half-conspiratorial look, staring after the tall, incredibly elegant Christine as she glided out of the room. ''How can we communicate properly when she's always attempting to take a rise out of me?''

"I'm sure we love her all the same,'' Mitch offered smoothly, staring at a beautiful, very showy orchid, its colours a combination of crimson, purple and pink. Wunnamurra had such an orchid right on its doorstep. Its name was Christine.

They had been airborne some twenty minutes when Mitch received the message that a vehicle was overturned on a bush road some forty plane-kilometres north-east of Wunnamurra station. Could he land and take a look at the scene? If there were critically injured people could he relay an immediate message to the Flying Doctor? If the occupants weren't so bad could he fly them back to Koomera Crossing, where an ambulance and a crew from the Bush Hospital would be waiting?

"Never a dull moment!'' Mitch remarked, shooting Christine a keen look. "I'll drop altitude. Keep your eyes peeled.''

Christine nodded, anxious to do all she could.

They had no difficulty finding the site. On a straight stretch of road the vehicle, a four-wheel drive, had come to grief.

"Thank God the wind is in the right direction," Mitch remarked, peering down at the rugged red landscape.

"You're going to attempt to land?" Christine too stared down at the vast plains that shimmered away to the horizon. Whirlwinds swayed and danced in the distance. The quivering mirage created an enticing chain of cool blue lagoons that many an explorer had trudged towards. Lakes that didn't exist. Empty and remote, the Never Never wasn't the best place to break down.

"I'll circle. See what happens," Mitch muttered. "If there's no response from the ground I guess I'll have to. The road should be just wide enough. At least we've got a good long straight stretch."

"You don't know the camber of the road," she pointed out, her tone betraying her edginess.

"You're not worried, are you?" He frowned, looking to her for a straight answer.

"No, Mitch. I'm as cool as a cucumber. Just like you. Of course I'm worried. There's certain criteria for landing on a road, even a bush road with not a soul on it. There's always a risk."

"Chrissy, darling, spare a thought. I'm the pilot," he said dryly. "Not you. I don't estimate a high risk. Leave it to me. I've seen the Flying Doctor's King Air—all five or six million dollars' worth, and weighing a good five tons— land in the most amazing places. You're talking skills. I'm not too bad myself."

A modest understatement. Mitch was a very fine pilot; he had to be. She knew that.

Rule One when travelling in the Outback: wait with your vehicle.

As they circled the site to make any survivors of the accident aware, a woman suddenly lurched up from the scant shade of a stunted, lifeless-looking shrub, her whole body language showing her distress. She lifted both arms above her head to acknowledge them before pointing back to the vehicle, then cantered to one side to indicate the driver was unable to get out.

"Doesn't look good," Mitch muttered. "I'm going down. Hold tight. It could be a little rough. Life insurance paid up?"

"Not funny, Mitch."

"You've lost your sense of humour away from the bush."

"You might too, if you hit a few potholes," she warned, responding to the taunt.

"Pray," he advised.

They were lined up for the bush runway, gear down by this stage. She knew she was a little panicky, and tried desperately to contain it. She wondered what conditions were like on the ground. There were whirlwinds ahead on the sweeping plains. But Mitch knew his job. She'd been very cosseted lately, she told herself wryly, travelling first class in jumbos.

It was a very impressive bit of flying. Without a jolt Mitch landed Marjimba's Beech Baron dead square on the hot and dusty bush road with, as she discovered when they climbed out, less than two feet to spare on either side of the plane's wheels before the verge sheared off into rubble.

"I had no idea you were that good." Her voice was droll.

"Keep the compliments for later," he clipped. "Let's assess what we're in for."

"Right." She grimaced, uncertain of what they'd find.

They'd barely started to move when panic really did set in. A herd of red kangaroos, up until then camouflaged by the thick mounds of spinifex where they'd been having their naps, suddenly popped up and began bounding here, there and everywhere on their powerful hind legs, muscular tails curved aloft, acting as balance. They hopped with ease up the slight gradient onto the road, displaying their usual considerable curiosity.

Once, chasing brumbies on motorbikes, she and Kyall had clocked the big male 'roos at sixty kilometres per hour. Presumably this lot had been spooked by the roar of the plane's engines and its astonishing presence on their territory.

"Get behind the vehicle," Mitch shouted to the woman, at the same time making a strong grab for Christine and hauling her back under the wing.

"Stay there," he ordered. "Goofy bloody things! God knows what they'll do next."

If it weren't so serious she would have laughed. She ignored Mitch's order. Head down, she darted behind him to the side of the road, where he bent to pick up a handful of large pebbles.

"Go on, then—pelt them," he snapped when he saw her.

"Pelt them yourself." With a rush of adrenalin, Christine took aim.

Neither of them, with all their childhood practice, had ever been known to miss. The whizzing pebbles found their solid targets as they bounded back and forth, but as the stones hit and then clattered to the road the kangaroos showed they weren't all that stupid. They began keeping out of range.

To start with, they could damage the plane, she thought. There were quite a few adult males, standing six feet and weighing around one hundred pounds out there, but the big fella, the leader, had to be at least seven feet tall and considerably heavier. They could surround them. Prevent a take-off. It would have been humorous—their antics *were* entertaining—except kangaroos were highly unpredictable.

To add to the general confusion the elderly woman had

entered the fray, yelling her head off and pitching a few pebbles that accidentally hit Mitch.

"To hell with this!" Mitch shouted. "I'm off before I get stoned by the old girl. Hold the fort. I'm going to fire off a few shots."

He made short work of getting his hands on the .22 rifle inside the plane, firing a few rounds to puncture the air. That put the kangaroos into another spin. It was quite a spectacle to see them bound off in a group for the wide open spaces, following up Big Red, who'd had just about enough of the rain of pebbles and the cracking gunshots.

"Thank God for that!" Mitch said laconically, stroking his chin. "It wouldn't surprise me if the 'roos were the cause of the accident. The driver may have taken fright and careened off the road."

Which was exactly what had happened, the wiry grey-haired woman told them disgustedly. She was well into her sixties but with something very spry about her. She had a darkening bruise beneath one of her otherwise bright eyes, but she appeared okay if a little excitable.

"Thank the good Lord you're here," she said fervently, blessing herself. "He always proves Himself, you know. "'Course, Clarry and I are a couple of the faithful. I'm Gemmima, by the way. Mima to Clarry. How in the world did you land that big plane on this narrow road?"

"As best I could, ma'am." Mitch gave her a smile. "We'd better take a look at Clarry. That's your husband?"

"He's not me toy boy, love." Gemmima's voice was full of humour. She started to walk alongside Mitch and Christine as they headed swiftly towards the vehicle.

"He's been slipping in and out of consciousness," she told them. "Concussed, I'd say, or God forbid he's had a bit of a heart attack. I dunno. He hit his head badly on the windscreen. I climbed out. He couldn't." She started to wring her hands, making a curious wailing sound. "Poor old Clarry! I told him to wait until the 'roos left the road, but he decided to make a dash for it."

"How are you going to get Clarry out?" Christine asked Mitch beneath her breath.

"I don't know yet. Depends what condition he's in. I might have to drag him."

"Could we right the vehicle? Bounce it? Rock it?"

"I don't know that either." He looked grim.

"You have no idea?"

"Listen, I'm open to suggestions," he said testily.

"Okay. Okay."

"It might be possible," he mused. "It hasn't canted that much. By the time you throw in your considerable body-weight..."

"Funny." They were sparring like in the old days.

When they looked in the vehicle a small gasp broke from Christine's lips. It was obvious that when the accident had happened Clarry had been pitched forward over the steering wheel, cracking his head and face into the windscreen. His forehead looked red raw, a mess of scrapes. He was older than Gemmima by a good few years, or appeared to be— old-timers exploring the Outback, not fully aware there could be an accident just waiting around the bend.

Along this stretch wild camels roamed. They moved in large groups and they too could cause big problems for the unwary tourist, station-bred Christine well knew.

"He's out of it, poor devil," Mitch said, making a swift examination. As a cattleman on a remote station he'd found it advisable to complete first aid and paramedic courses, simply to be able to cope with accidents when they happened. Looking after his men was a big responsibility. "Breathing's a bit laboured. His neck looks okay. A bad concussion, I'd say. He was lucky. He's a bit on the frail side. I can't do much for him except get him back to Koomera Crossing ASAP. Less time than the Flying Doctor would take to get here anyway.''

He looked across at Christine's alert face. ''Meantime, you get on the radio and relay the message. They need the crew standing by. Tell them concussion, possible heat exhaustion. Head injury, but it doesn't look significant.''

Christine broke into a run and after a minute Gemmima ran after her.

By the time they returned Mitch had performed a minor miracle. He had Clarry lying out on the road, with a rug that must have been in the vehicle spread beneath him.

Gemmima let out a loud whoop. ''Gee, that's great! Are yah dreamin', Clarry?'' She stared down at the man on the rug.

''No, he's conscious—aren't you, Clarry?'' Mitch bent over the man. ''Just doing a bit of drifting.''

''What happened?'' Clarry suddenly asked, sounding very dazed but coherent.

''We got beat up by a lot of kangaroos.'' Gemmima had her husband's trembling hand firmly between hers. ''Or the car did. But God's turned His face to us, Clarry. We've got these angels here.''

Mitch gave her his beautiful white smile. ''No one has ever called us angels before.''

''You've got wings, haven't yah? Further, I have a feelin' you do lots of good things.'' Gemmima squinted up at Christine. ''You sure are a good-looking girl. A bit tall, but I kinda like it. That plait of yours is like a rope. I used to have hair like that, believe it or not. I bet your husband loves to brush it. Reckon you're newly-weds.''

Christine blushed hotly, not trusting herself to look at the sardonic Mitch. ''I have to own up, Gemmima, he's not my husband.''

"Soon will be, if I'm not mistaken." Gemmima squatted down by her husband, who smiled at her tenderly. "I can see it in your faces. I know these things. Clarry could tell yah if he wasn't so shook up."

"I think you're a woman who puts a positive spin on everything, Gemmima," Mitch said in a smooth, pleasant voice. "Now, I want you to go ahead with Chris. I'm going to get Clarry to the plane."

"Good on yah!" said Gemmima, rising unaided and taking Christine's hand. "He's a real Outback hero. No wonder you're in love with him." She gave Christine a warm smile. "I'm goin' to be praying for you two."

"Make it a thousand Our Fathers," Mitch suggested. "How are you feeling now, Clarry?" he asked as the women moved off.

"Gettin' there." Clarry grimaced.

"Not too good?"

"I'm seein' two of yah, not one."

"Concussion," Mitch said, not wanting to worry the man. "Now, I'm going to lift you and carry you back to the plane. Tell me if you're in any pain."

"I'll be okay, if you just take it easy," Clarry maintained. "Don't reckon I could walk."

"You don't have to." Mitch gave him a wry grin. "Just relax and enjoy the ride."

CHAPTER THREE

UNLIKE Wunnamurra, the reigning queen of homesteads, Marjimba Station hadn't changed all that much since Mitch's grandfather's day, Christine thought. Captain Douglas Claydon, awarded the Military Medal for bravery in the field, had returned home from war in the North African desert to marry his faithful Kathleen and add an extra wing. The new wing was to house his parents while he and Kathleen took over the main house to raise a family. Douglas had hoped for much needed sons, to love and take pride in. They would help him run Marjimba Station, while his daughters would delight him with their accomplishments and marry well, preferably into landed families like themselves. What he and Kathleen got was one fine son, always his favourite, and four clever daughters who lived in their brother's shadow but did go on to marry into suitable pastoral families. This had created a powerful network through kinship of landed people who could depend on one another through thick and thin, people who quietly helped one another out when times were tough.

The Claydons and their extended family were universally liked and respected. Family partnerships had been formed to ensure prosperity for them all, new ventures undertaken to carry the cattle chain through the lean times. They had invested heavily in mining and mineral exploration, then cotton, taking a lead from Christine's own family, the McQueens. The name of the game was diversification for both families, though they had one powerful thing in common. They loved the land with a passion.

Christine stood in the burnished sunlight of the driveway, with the rush of green and gold budgerigar overhead, looking at the rambling white homestead that was the Claydon family home. It was set in a grove of magnificent date palms and fiery Outback flora. Unlike Wunnamurra, which was two-storeyed, Marjimba was a large low-lying building. Two wings jutted out at an angle from the original central structure to form what looked like three separate pyramids with wraparound verandahs. All three sections were reached by a short flight of stone steps. Mitch, she knew, had had the whole west wing to himself since he'd turned fourteen and been judged a man.

The first time they'd made love had been in his bedroom after a ball the Claydons had hosted. She remembered the whole experience as though it were yesterday. The white heat, the hot blood, the thudding heart. Pure desire. She held it all fast in the citadel of her heart. The memory would never go away; like haunting melodies remained in the mind.

She had easily been the most noticeable girl there that night. She'd said it was because of her height. Mitch had said it was because she was just so darn beautiful.

"Your eyes are like liquid sapphires; your skin has the lustre of a pearl; your mouth is as red as rubies." He had waxed lyrical as his desire increased. "I can see the cleft between your breasts, now the flush on your cheeks!"

Mitch! He'd been giddy with love for her. Her heart in his hands.

Her ballgown had been the same colour as her eyes, a deep blue silk-taffeta, daringly strapless with a tight bodice, tiny waist and a wonderful billowing skirt. Her grandmother, Ruth, had actually let her wear some family jewellery—more for showing off the family possessions than from affection—a perfect sapphire as big as a walnut on a diamond chain. There had been pendant earrings to match, that when she had danced bounced against her cheeks, sending out chinks of light. Even her mother had seemed deeply impressed, and her father content to put his arm around her and kiss her cheek, murmuring, "My beautiful girl!"

Mitch had been her date. Mitch had always been her date. And that night she'd fought such a physical battle against temptation, desperate to behave as expected of her when all her senses and those she hadn't even known she possessed stirred unbidden. That night Mitch had become her first lover. He'd given her the sexual rapture she'd thought she couldn't live without but very sadly did.

Her mental images were so luminous she could have moaned aloud: Mitch holding her passionately in the dark—"I can't, Chris, I can't, I can't. I can't wait any longer. I love you. I'm mad about you. I've got protection. I promise I'll never let anything bad happen to you. My love. My love."

The agony in his voice had rendered her incandescent, both of them gasping and stumbling, blindly, intensely kissing, hoping, hoping to reach the west wing and his bedroom before someone discovered them. No one who hadn't experienced passionate love could imagine the force of it. If you wanted someone, truly wanted someone, you were lost. If you loved them as she had loved Mitch they entered your psyche.

She had returned his fevered kisses, pressing her body cased in its beautiful gown into his, deliberately inciting him so he hauled her onto the bed. She had felt the thrilling physical sensations in her breasts, in her stomach, the knife-edge between her legs, the strong pull on her womb.

Mitch—his mouth moving all over her face, her neck, the swell of her breasts. She remembered the smell of his skin, the taste of him, his tongue caressing hers. At nineteen, two years older than she, he was the most skilful lover, expertly playing her nerves and sinews like the strings on a violin.

It had been ecstasy and terror. An extravagant blend of both. A giant leap to another level of their extraordinary relationship begun when they were children. In the end she couldn't have stopped him even if she had wanted to. She'd known he couldn't stop himself. It had been delirium. Her first sexual experience. The one against which all others had been judged. And found wanting.

She didn't know whether to laugh or weep. She could simply say she was a one-man woman...

"Say, what's wrong?" Mitch demanded. He'd been assembling her baggage and placing it up on the verandah. Now he came alongside, struck by her preoccupation with the west wing.

"Good question." She lowered her thick eyelashes before he caught any residual emotion in her gaze.

"Looks like you were thrown by a few memories?" he remarked tersely. As youngsters they'd prided themselves on being able to read each other's thoughts.

"Okay, so it was the most exciting night of my life." She didn't attempt to hide her patently obvious thoughts. "The first time we made love."

"Chrissy, Chrissy, is that supposed to upset me?" he asked, leaning back against the Jeep and jamming his hands in his pockets. "I'm quite sure you've enjoyed a good sex-life these past years."

"Me?" She gave a little self-mocking grimace. "I live like a nun."

"Not believeable, kiddo," he clipped, raking her with his eyes. "Unless you've totally changed. The least you can do is show me what you've learned."

Her heart twisted at his insolence. Even simple friendship seemed to be out of the question. "Correct me if I'm wrong, but didn't you give me to understand I'd better back off?"

"We're grown-ups, aren't we?" he countered, staring her down. "I don't get a lot of fun way out here, Chrissy. What I meant was that you'll never get me to the altar again."

"I didn't get you there the first time," she reminded him tartly.

"Now that's a rotten answer. You women are so cruel. You were seriously contemplating it. We made love every time we could. In barns, around corners, every bend of the creek, our lily pond. It was love, wasn't it?"

She looked straight into his blissful blue eyes. "It was more like a freefall through space."

He didn't move, but glanced away abruptly, adjusting the tilt of his akubra on his gold-fire hair. "The symbolism, my dear Chrissy, isn't lost on me. But if you'd like to sneak into my room one night while you're here, I'm sure we can work something out. It's just that we'll never be what we were again."

She shoved on her sunglasses. "I agree. I won't be tempted either."

"What, you're in denial?"

She had started walking; now she halted abruptly, coming within inches of his taunting face.

"How come you can't commit to anyone?"

"Spoken by the woman who dumped me." Languidly he pushed a stray silky lock behind her ear. "I was only having you on, Chrissy. You won't get your head on my pillow again. Never!"

"Who says?" she challenged, holding the blue gaze.

"I say."

"Listen, Mitch Claydon, don't ever use a sentence that ends in 'never' with me."

He gave a low whistle, then his marvellous smile. "You know, Chrissy, it's really weird, but you sound just like you used to when you were about sixteen."

"And you were already in love with me."

"True." His eyes darkened to turquoise and she felt his instant withdrawal. "I've been through that once. I don't plan on doing it twice. Now, let's go inside before this conversation starts getting really rough."

Julanne Claydon loved having Christine in the house. She'd been badly missing her daughter, India, presently living in London, but Christine was surely the next best thing.

Christine knew life could be very lonely for station women, so she did all the things she knew Julanne loved. They took long walks together, or drove to a cool shady picnic spot beside a water lily-filled lagoon. They enjoyed being quiet together or chatting companionably. They listened to music together—Christine had brought over a whole range of CDs—and they played chess just like in the old days.

Both of them loved games of strategy. Christine, to whom winning wasn't as important as enjoying the game, was still amused by Julanne's competitiveness. She never gave up. Afterwards they always had tea, accompanied by a slice of delicious freshly baked cake. Christine always said if she stayed much longer she'd get fat.

"Do racehorses put on weight?" Julanne would reply.

"She's every bit as down to earth and sunny-natured as when she was a child," Julanne confided to Mitch one evening, when he called to say goodnight. "Success hasn't gone to her head at all! She enjoys the same old things: having dinner with the family, catching up on all the gossip, the latest news about mutual friends, who's had a baby who's expecting one, the inevitable losses in families—all the sorts of things India never really enjoys talking about much.''

''India was always preoccupied with Kyall,'' Mitch pointed out dryly. He watched his mother, glowingly serene, as she brushed out the thick, curling, sun-streaked blonde hair that had once been as golden as his own. ''Kyall was the centre of her life.''

''I blame Ruth for that.'' Julanne brushed harder. ''And myself too, of course. I failed India by allowing her to believe she had a chance.''

Mitch slumped into an armchair sighing. ''Mum, no one had a chance as long as there was Sarah. Those two were made for each other.''

''I know that.'' Julanne spoke more calmly. ''And what about you two? You and Chris? You're always sparring with each other. She's been here two days and the air fairly crackles.''

''That's when I get to see her,'' he said in a mock injured voice. ''She's been keeping you company mostly.''

''Yes, isn't she sweet?'' Julanne smiled. ''Don't think I'm going to keep her chained to my side, but she's such fun. She brought heaps of photographs for me to see. She's got some wonderful fashion shots, and photographic-type shots of just her face. She knew I'd love them, but it's all part of the trade to her. They don't mean much to Christine. Vanity has never been her problem.''

''She got too much of a drubbing as a girl,'' Mitch pointed out with a flash of anger. ''I don't like to think about the way her mother and Ruth gave her such a hard time.''

''No, it was pretty bad.'' Julanne groped around for her glasses. ''No wonder she sprouted wings and flew away.''

"She also left me, Mum," Mitch reminded her, spotting his mother's reading glasses and handing them to her. "I thought I'd never get over it. My one and only love. Isn't that pitiful? She abandoned me so she could show the rest of the world how beautiful she is."

"It doesn't sound like you've found a cure?" Julanne eyed her adored son with open sympathy.

"You know darn well I haven't. Which doesn't mean I'm thrilled to have her here."

"Oh?" Julanne's full-throated mezzo sounded highly sceptical.

"Don't look at me like that. I know how you feel about Chris, but she's going to go away again, Mum. Don't kid yourself or get your hopes too high. This will all be too tame for her. She's lived a very glamorous lifestyle. She's told us any number of times she adores New York. She's done what thousands of women would only dream of doing."

"Be that as it may!" Julanne murmured vaguely, going to a drawer of her bureau and removing a sheaf of glossy photographs. She extended them to her son." Take a look at those. I know you want to. It seems to me there are two Christines. The public Christine— the supermodel moving with all the beautiful people—and the real Christine. The one who loves the land, who loves horses and rides like the wind. I'm sure she could leave all the fancy clothes and the wonderful jewellery behind tomorrow. She's perfectly happy in her old gear."

"Old gear?" Mitch mocked, pausing to stare down at a photograph for a moment. What a luscious mouth Chrissy had. "You mean the tight designer jeans, the sexy little gauzy blouses and the crisp striped shirts? The trendy T-shirts with the tiny sleeves and fancy logos across the front calling attention to her beautiful breasts? She's all woman now, Mum. Forget the boyish look she used to cultivate to annoy her mother.''

''You'd think they were trying to break something in her,'' Julanne mused. ''Ruth McQueen was the strangest woman I ever encountered or ever expect to. She had so much influence on poor Enid.''

''Poor Enid, nothing!'' Mitch exclaimed. He was forever loyal to Christine, and there was nothing he could do about it. ''It's a sad state of affairs when you have to escape your own mother.''

''It happens,'' Julanne breathed. ''Wonderful, aren't they?'' She referred to the photographs. ''The camera just loves her.''

''It's her cheekbones. She'll have them until she's an old, old lady. She'll go away, Mum,'' Mitch found himself saying again bleakly.

''Are you sure you don't want to stop her?''

''What, and go through it all again? We were so close, but there's a big divide between us now.''

''Seems to me on your side, my darling.'' Julanne studied her son closely.

''I don't trust her,'' Mitch confessed, brilliant-eyed.

''Gracious!'' Julanne waved her hands in distress. ''A more trustworthy young woman I can't imagine. You're too hard on Chris.''

''No, she was too cruel to me,'' Mitch corrected. ''Chris made certain promises. I believed them. When she took off she left me in the wilderness. She's not going to get a chance to do it again.''

''I never knew you suffered from the sin of pride,'' Julanne said slowly.

''Well, I do.'' Mitch rose slowly to his full height, dwarfing his mother who was above average height.

"You're a lovely-looking woman," he said gently. "Sunlit."

"Why, thank you, darling!" Julanne flushed with pleasure. "I try to keep myself looking nice."

"Well, it's paid off." He bent and kissed her cheek. "Would it be okay if I borrowed Chris for a few hours in the morning?"

"What do you plan to do?" Julanne's face brightened with interest.

"A few of us are going in search of Lightning. He's taken at least two of our mares and one of our fillies. Bart saw him running yesterday with his harem near Mulagimbi Waterhole."

"You want to catch him?"

"We're going to try to," he said wryly. "I don't mind the brumby herds remaining in the wild, but Lightning has real quality blood. He's got good breeding and it shows. Probably his mother ran off to join the wild horses when she was in foal. Lightning's very strong, and very sure-footed. He's much taller than most of the wild horses, and he'll make a good stockhorse if handled properly. Chris might like to come along. She'd have loved it in the old days."

"I'm sure she hasn't changed a bit," Julanne said loyally, pleased Mitch had thought of it. "I wouldn't want her to take a nasty tumble, though."

"She won't," Mitch told her dryly. "I caught sight of her riding at sunset. She's lost none of her old skills."

"Then go with my blessing," said Julanne, her maternal heart brimming with hope.

He caught up with Christine as she was off to bed. "Got a minute?"

All the time in the world, Mitch, she thought. Part of her

wanted badly, so very badly, to tell him that, but she just knew what his reaction would be. "Sure," she managed casually.

His hair was pure gold in the light of the chandelier. She wanted to put out her hand and ruffle it. How complicated their relationship had become. She'd better accustom herself to it.

"I thought you might like a bit of action?"

She laughed aloud, even though her heart quaked. "Is this some sort of trick question?"

"Surely sex can't be on your lovely mind?" he chided, looking up at her with exaggerated surprise.

"Of all people why with you? Haven't you totally rejected me?" She couldn't relax around him. Every pulse throbbed.

"Not necessarily. Only if you're going for the magnolia satin wedding dress and the lace veil."

At his words, totally unexpected, she stepped back in time. "I can't believe you remembered that."

"Don't worry. I've forgotten nothing," he said a shade harshly. "You spent many hours telling me what you were going to wear when we got married."

"I meant it." She sighed, sad and vulnerable. "We were so young."

"Weren't we ever?" Irony sprang from his lips. "Thank God we'll never be that young again. I would have given up everything for you. These days when I'm ready to get married I'll have an airtight pre-nuptial agreement drawn up."

She watched those sea-coloured eyes, the hard glitter in them. "You're too cynical, that's your trouble, Mitch. Whatever happened to Susan Gilroy?"

"Zsa-Zsa?" Now he did smile, his mouth relaxed and curvy.

"She's the one you fitted in between Dee Marshall and Casey Thomas, if I remember rightly."

"I'm amazed you kept yourself so well informed."

"Actually, it was Kyall who filled me in when I pressed him for news of you from time to time."

He gave a nonchalant shrug. "Ah, well, we've both had our affairs. Mine perhaps not as well documented as yours. At least I haven't managed one with a rock star."

"He's not a rock star. I've already told you, he's a soap star. And he's a very nice guy."

"Afternoon TV's hottest hero."

"Take comfort. It's not serious. So where's the action?" Christine moved the conversation onto neutral ground.

He made a business of snapping to attention. "I think it's something you'll enjoy. A few of us plan on going in search of a very classy brumby stallion called Lightning. He's got thoroughbred blood, no question. Lightning has already taken a couple of our mares and a filly to join his harem."

"And you think he'll make a good station horse?"

"I know so. Also, I'd like to hold onto what mares he's been kind enough to leave us. Lightning thinks he's king of the plains. He's magnificent to watch. We've even spotted him running with the station horses. Only one thing I need to know—do you think you're up to it?"

She gave an excited nod, lovely colour sweeping up into her cheeks. "Does anyone forget how to ride a horse?"

He rested his hands against the polished mahogany banister, staring up at her. Behind them hung a large gilded Georgian mirror that gave back their reflections. A study in gold and ebony. "I'm talking a hard gallop, and we might have to cross a couple of creeks."

She pursed her full mouth. "Thank you, Mitch, for your vote of confidence, but I'm as good for the chase as I ever was. You know that. That's why you're asking me along. I thought I detected you spying on me from the hill country.''

''Spying? Never!'' he lied easily. ''I was killing two birds with the one stone. Checking you out and giving instructions to a couple of stockmen mustering the area.''

''I see. Well, I'd love to come, Mitch. What time?''

''We'll mount up at first light. We need to get underway before it gets too hot. If you haven't got good protective gear I'll find you some. It could be rough going.''

''I'll need gloves and chaps. I want the big chestnut gelding I rode this afternoon. Wellington.''

''Anything else?'' he asked dryly.

''Not that I can think of at this minute,'' she returned sweetly.

''No friendly goodnight kiss?'' Burnt gold lashes hooded his brilliant eyes.

The nerves in her body twitched in shock. What was he trying to do to her? ''You're a tease if ever there was one!'' She spoke lightly, though she knew a kind of crisis was looming.

''What a label!'' he scoffed. ''Who said I'm teasing anyway?''

''Am I hearing right? Can it be that you still care?'' She visibly trembled as his eyes drifted across her. She felt her body come alive, breasts swelling against the silk of her shirt, delicate tips stiffening in instant arousal.

He noted all this with perverse satisfaction. ''I don't. But you are beautiful.'' He revelled in her arousal. Clung to it with a strange vehemence.

''Damaged pride?'' she suggested.

''Ahh!'' He moved up to her, pressing his fingers to her mouth, silencing her. ''You really are one arrogant lady.''

"I don't mean to be." Her cushiony mouth pulsed from the pressure of those fingers.

"And you a McQueen?"

With all that implied. "Reardon," she corrected sharply.

"As close to a McQueen as one can get." He shrugged, his hands moving to her shoulders.

She stood perfectly still as his fingers began to play with her dark abundant hair just as they'd used to. "I'm over you, Chrissy," he said, disturbingly soft. "God help me, but I am."

"Prove it." She wasn't such a fool that she couldn't feel the pounding weight of sexual tension, the tiny tremble in those strong fingers.

"Letting go comes hard for you, doesn't it?" he accused, taking her slender throat in his hands.

"Why would you want to kiss a woman who's meant nothing but trouble?" she challenged, moving in even closer. Her need for him was so keenly, powerfully, physical it was unbearable.

"I think of it as fighting fire with fire," he murmured, though there was nothing remotely tender in his expression. "You can keep your eyes open, if you like."

Nothing could stop this, once begun.

It sounded simple enough. Keep your eyes open. It wasn't. As he lowered his head her eyelids involuntarily closed, long jet-black lashes fanning her cheeks. She shuddered as a violent rush of exhilaration came for her, swamping her in its pelting torrents. Drowning her.

She fought for air, determined she wouldn't allow him the luxury of making a fool of her. But the warmth and weight of his marvellous curvy mouth came down over hers.

Resistance was futile. The years of long denial were over. She let herself go, assailed by the clean scent of his breath, his mating tongue, the wonderful male fragrance of his hair and skin. It had stayed with her for years.

Stars burst. Whole galaxies. The full rush of blind sex.

For Mitch it was meant to be an exercise in control, a mocking kiss that would convey to her he was no longer in her power. Only the kiss with its strict limitations quickly changed character. It turned to passion and a kind of fury. Passion that came out in force, whipping layer after layer of his hard-won defences from him, leaving him totally exposed.

With an incoherent mutter he slipped his arm to her waist and hauled her into him. The whole length of their bodies fused—breast, waist, hip, thigh, long legs—as each tried desperately to meet the need to melt into the other. He compulsively plied the length of her back with his strong hand in a muted violence that had her arching her body still closer, head tilted back so he could kiss her more fully.

She wasn't aware how long they stood like that—an eternity?—mouth hungrily taking mouth as longing broke free of its hiding place.

As an outpouring of need it was staggering. How could a kiss capture so much territory? The flesh, with its undertow of hot pulsing blood and racing nerves; the chambers of the heart; the marrow.

When he released her it was to a white-hot ringing silence. as though both were shocked by the level of arousal a single kiss had detonated.

Christine found herself staring into his face, taut with desire, blue eyes blazing.

"I think your kisses always did frighten me," she whispered, incredibly moved.

"How?" His blue eyes scorched her.

"I used to think my soul passed into yours through my mouth," she confessed.

"Didn't it?" he asked tensely.

"It's possible, Mitch, to be frightened of too much emotion. To ache with you, without you, from you."

"So you're now trying to tell me you were frightened all those dark starry nights?" he asked explosively.

"I used to think I was so much in love with you that I would disappear."

His frown was bleak. "You never once said anything like that to me."

"I'm saying it now. There was terror in it, Mitch. I was so young and inexperienced. Passion is a fever. Feel my hand; feel my cheek." She offered her cheek to him, knowing without looking, toward the mirror her skin was incandescent with hot blood.

He didn't trust himself to obey, but he did. His lean fingers traced the curve of her cheek, drifted to the slope of her shoulder. He was deeply desirous to cup her breasts—he could see the erect nipples peaking against the silky shirt—only that would have been total surrender. They both would have understood she had won. He wasn't going to allow her that bitter victory.

"You taste exactly the same. Sweet on my tongue." He forced his hands to drop. He moved back from temptation. "You'd better go to bed, Chris." His tone was quiet, but clearly dismissive. "We have an early start in the morning."

"They say you never forget your first love," she murmured sadly.

"Or words to that effect." Deliberately he kept his tone cynical, when what he really thought was this: sometimes a man never learned to love more than once.

CHAPTER FOUR

ALL the time she was dressing, Christine had the stirring lines of "Banjo" Paterson's famous Outback poem, *The Man from Snowy River* running through her head. Brumby-running had a rich history in the nation, and Paterson's poem captured the full excitement of the chase. She'd seen many brumbies trapped in roughly made "yards" over the years, had participated in musters, but this was something different again.

Lightning, though he was wild, had good thoroughbred blood in him, Mitch had said. That meant he would be faster, probably much faster than any mounted stockman. Except Zena, Mitch's silver mare, had wings, and Wellington, her horse for the morning, was good for pace. Her excitement grew. The domestic horses enjoyed the chase as much as the riders. Station born and bred, Christine had been associated with horses for most of her life. And the brumbies had a mystique of their own. It was a marvellous sight to see them running in a herd. They were part of Outback culture and the best of them, all progeny of runaway or stolen station horses, had always been sought after.

This big black stallion, Lightning, was no exception. Helicopters and motorbikes had largely revolutionised station life, but horses, magnificent creatures that they were, were part of the nation's heritage, forever linked with the Outback and the Australian Light Horse at war. Christine knew she would have been bitterly disappointed had Mitch not asked her to join them on the chase. At least he acknowledged she fitted into some part of his world. The land was part of them both.

Six of them rode out: Mitch, Christine, Jack Cody, the new overseer, two of the top hands—"Smiley" Jensen, of the poker face, and Abe Lovell—and the station's finest aboriginal tracker, "Snowy" Moon, whose halo of ash-white curls made such a pleasing contrast with his dark chocolate skin.

All of them were fine horsemen, although Christine didn't take to Jack Cody, who had assumed the coveted job of station overseer from Dave Reed, when he'd retired with a handsome annuity after forty years of service to the Claydons and Marjimba Station. He had, however, come straight from a cattle station in the Territory, highly recommended as a capable overseer.

Tall, good-looking in his way, and very fit, he was in his mid-thirties and divorced. His marriage had apparently crashed. He was respectful enough, but there was something Christine didn't like in the length and quality of his hazel gaze. She was tempted to say something to Mitch, but decided against it. She didn't really want to get Jack into trouble, but his gaze reminded her of the speculative stare of other men who had sexually propositioned her. Or longed to. She knew that look. The hardness behind it, the too intimate lop-sided grin.

He continued to stare when he thought she wasn't looking, ceasing only when Mitch, who had been giving last-minute instructions to Snowy, rode back to her side.

"Before I forget, I've had word from Sarah," Mitch told her. "The hospital has released Clarry." He referred to the elderly man they had rescued in the desert. "They won't be resuming their journey. He suffered a mild heart attack as well as concussion. Gemmima's flying him home. Both of them send their regards. They want to keep in touch."

"Where are they based?" Christine, seated on Wellington, who needed a good rider to control him, adjusted the red bandanna around her neck. It would be too tight when the heat mounted.

"Adelaide."

Mitch allowed his eyes to fall on her. He was seduced all over again. She had ruled his dreams the night before to the extent that he'd woken once, heart pounding, thinking she was naked beside him. Now, in the glimmering light of dawn, she was the picture of health and vitality.

She wasn't wearing a scrap of make-up. She didn't need it. Just a touch of rosy lipgloss, most probably to protect the sensitive skin of her mouth. Her beautiful springy dark hair was drawn back into a plaited rope, and her skin and eyes glowed. She was a real beauty, as opposed to artificial, her sapphire eyes arresting against the jet-black of brows and lashes. Christine Reardon. His downfall.

She was smiling as she answered. "I expect they're very grateful to you for rescuing their vehicle as well. It must have cost an arm and a leg."

"How did you know?" He wasn't someone who broadcast his good deeds.

"Your mother told me. She always wants me to know how kind and generous you are."

"It's called being a mother," he complained, making an affectionate low clicking sound with his tongue. His mount, the splendid, very agile silver-grey mare Zena, responded. She moved off obediently, quite happy with her stablemate the big chestnut Wellington alongside.

Even at this early hour the mirage was abroad. It painted waves of blue fire at the feet of the distant hump-backed hills. The hills looked close, but Christine knew they were twenty miles to the north-west. The air was incredibly sweet, scented by the trillion fuzzy golden balls of the flow-ering acacias that dotted the landscape.

How I love the scent of wattle, she thought, breathing in deeply. It's the smell of my homeland. The scent of the bush. My country. How I've missed it. She risked a glance at Mitch. God, he was beautiful! Happiness surged. On a scale of one to ten she was on Cloud Eleven. She was even hopeful she could win him back.

Forty minutes on and they were on the edge of a chain of lakes the Claydons called the Blue Billabongs: areas of oasis on the semi-arid desert fringe. Here the waters were a curious pearly green, but the lakes took their name from the exquisite dark blue and violet water lilies, with their masses of yellow stamens, that were reflected in the tranquil waters.

At this magical hour the air was alive with the extraor-dinary Outback bird life, especially along the lines of the creeks and billabongs. Budgerigar, zebra finches, the red-capped robins and the orange chats, brilliant lorikeets, sul-phur-crested cockatoos, clouds of geese and water birds, blue kingfishers and, through the breaks in the silver-grey eucalypts, glimpses of the elegant brolgas stepping deli-cately along the sandy banks.

The spinifex that had stood silver against the dawn light now caught fire with the rising sun. It turned for long mo-ments a fiery red before blazing gold. The sky above was already bright blue and cloudless as the sun established its supremacy. It gave Christine a feeling of wholeness, com-pleteness, she had never experienced anywhere else.

"You look remarkably happy," Mitch said, feeling the self-same peace. They were riding so close the sides of their mounts almost swished.

"You can't imagine how I've missed this," she admitted with a voluptuous sigh. "This is what makes me tick."

One dark golden eyebrow shot up. "That's odd—I thought you'd find it pretty hard away from the glamorous capitals of the world."

"Do I look like I'm finding it hard?" she flashed back.

She rode beautifully. Back erect. "Oh, well, while on holiday one has to make the most of it," he mused.

"How can I be on holiday? This is where I was born. This my world as well as yours, Mitch Claydon. Thank you very much. 'Here I am, homeward from my wandering. Here I am homeward and my heart is healed'."

"I wish I could say the same for mine," he said dryly.

Instinctively she turned to him. "There'll always be a bond between us, Mitch. You might as well accept that."

"Oh, I do!" He shrugged. "But sometimes it catches me by surprise. Like last night."

"I don't regret it, do you?" Not those minutes of rapturous abandonment.

"That remains to be seen. Essentially, I can't afford to get too close to you ever again. It's called self-preservation. You can understand that, surely? After all, you're bound to do the same old thing. You'll go away."

"Could you consider I'm tired of being Christine Reardon, public figure?" she asked.

"You mean you're tossing up between the idea of retiring or perhaps moving to the silver screen? You've got a head start. You've got yourself an American accent when others have to study it."

"You can't help acquiring an accent when you spend a lot of time in a country," she said reasonably. "Besides, I like an American accent—though there are plenty of them. Mine's more cosmopolitan."

"It should come in handy, should you make the move."

She ignored the bitter mockery. "Hey, can we ride along peacefully?"

"Sure. I want your holiday to be a good one."

She lifted a hand, whispered behind it. "I hate you, Mitch."

"I hate you too, only you get me excited." His gaze sparkled as it settled on her mouth.

"That's the intention." Her whole body was brushed with heat.

"Tell me again when we're alone."

"So you can put me in my place?"

"Now, Chrissy, that only makes good sense."

By mid-morning they had made their first sighting of Lightning and his harem, along the beautiful wild banks of the Blue Billabongs—to the aboriginals on the station a home of mystical beings. Flashes of ebony, bay, bright chestnuts and creams were caught in the dancing light through the thick screening of trees.

Mitch, his expression exhilarated, a little taut, lifted a hand to signal they were off.

Where there were chases there was always danger.

Brumbies were cunning. They tended to see station horses and riders a split second before they themselves were spotted, their hearing being vastly superior to humans'. It was virtually impossible to swoop upon a brumby. The wild horse had to be outrun, outclassed or penned up in some way.

They had to consider the best strategy for containing this stallion. In this landscape a lignum swamp or ravine. It was no easy task, roping a brumby, anyway, whether from the ground or, harder yet, from a galloping horse.

Lightning, the brumby leader, was showing his thoroughbred blood. Just like a racehorse, from a standing start he bounded into a gallop, instantly activating the wild herd. Christine watched as the brumbies scattered into the scrub,

manes whipping, coats sleek and gleaming as they flashed
through the timber, heading for what lay ahead—eroded hill
country and beyond that the open plain.

They were off!

Wild gallops were nothing new to Christine. Many a time
she had taken part in bush races, but she had never been
able to outrun Mitch. Now Mitch, a superb horseman, was
already clear in front, his mare, Zena, incredibly fit and
eager for the chase. Jack Cody, the overseer, galloped past
her actually taking the time to flash her a triumphant grin
that held more than a hint of leer. The rest of the party
were hot on her tail.

Without weight to carry the brumbies were holding their
lead, except for two mothers with foals who dropped back
as the rest of the herd forged ahead. The riders ignored
them. It was only the black stallion they were after.

A fallen branch as big as a hurdle loomed ahead of
Christine, who had decided on a shortcut as part of her
tactics. It reared out of the scrub giving her a split second
of panic before she sent Wellington soaring over it. She
already knew the big chestnut was a clean jumper. The
gelding didn't hesitate, relishing the challenge.

More hurdles confronted her, big spreading branches, but
she rode hell for leather, ducking the low-growing rungs of
the mulga, keeping Mitch not all that far ahead, locked in
her vision. Finally she burst out of the timber, her taut rear
slamming hard into leather, breasts rising and falling, skin
slick with sweat, booted feet feeling weightless in the stirrups. She was utterly intoxicated with the charge. A great
flight of budgerigar formed a green and gold canopy over
her, their antics keeping time with her mount.

Some of the inferior horses of Lightning's harem, fillies
and mares, were starting to fall back. The riding party galloped on past them, intent on capturing Lightning, who ran

with the best of the colts—colts that in the normal course of events would one day fight him for control of the harem.

Mitch was a crack hand with the rope, but the little mob was going like the wind. The trail she had blazed on her own brought Christine out in front of all the men, including the hard-riding Cody. Wildlife darted for cover. Kangaroos and wallabies and wandering emus, those great flightless birds, pulled out their own dazzling turn of speed. The creek's kingfishers and kookaburras, always in high spirits, chuckled at the chase, but the multitudes of sulphur-crested cockatoos adorning the trees like giant white flowers rose into the air, screeching indignantly at the galloping procession of horses.

As Christine approached Mitch at speed he indicated his intention to drive the herd towards a section of the eroded hills criss-crossed by low canyons. The wrong canyon and the brumbies would escape. The right one and they stood an excellent chance of capturing the muscular jet-coloured stallion. He had to stand seventeen hands. Proof of his good blood.

The others were thundering up to them, Snowy, the aboriginal tracker, calling out loudly and tossing his head in the direction of a particular rotund dome in the line of hump-backed hills. It glowed like a red-hot furnace in the blazing sun.

The colts were faltering. The mares had given up. The stallion was still thundering across the hard-baked sand, but as the riding party got into their line of battle, flanking the stallion, his headlong flight to escape was effectively funnelled towards the squat dome and its near neighbour, a narrow pinnacle that rose considerably higher. A narrow ravine lay between, with only one entrance, its exit blocked by huge boulders.

The chase was over.

Inside the rock-strewn narrow canyon the stallion turned to confront them, rearing and tossing his head. He was snorting in the wildest, most intimidating fashion Christine had ever heard. No station horse could put on a war-like display like this. One powerful front leg struck the ground, pawing over and over, issuing a warning.

"Might be a bad one, boss," Snowy called to Mitch. "Mightn't be worth havin'. Got that look about 'im."

"Hell, Snowy, we've done our damnedest to corner him. Are you saying we should let him go?" Mitch's reply had an edge of exasperation, particularly as he was arriving at the same conclusion.

"Uneasy, boss." Snowy smiled grimly. "This guy a rogue. Look at da eyes. There's a debbil in them eyes."

"I agree." Christine's gaze was fixed on the stallion and his menacing attitude.

"He's aggressive, all right," Mitch muttered, knowing the stallion was trouble but loath to let him go free. "You don't reckon you could tame him, Snowy?" Snowy was a marvellous horse-handler. None better.

"Concerned him no good, boss. Could be a killer."

Christine spoke quietly. "Let him go, Mitch. I've got a bad feeling about this one."

That infuriated Jack Cody. "Bugger that!" he exploded, throwing Christine a look that said women were useless except for one thing. "If Snowy can't break him, I can."

Mitch wheeled Zena around, staring at the overseer. Jack had not been his choice. His father had appointed him. "I don't think I care for the prospect of your breaking him, Cody. I'm sure the stallion wouldn't like it either. We've got a bit of a problem here, though. Lightning is becoming a real menace. We can't possibly fence in our station horses. They're used to roaming a huge area. But I won't lose the two station mares."

"Why don't we collect them?" Christine suggested, riding quietly to Mitch's right. "Lightning will burn himself out."

"What would a woman know about horses?" Jack Cody challenged, eyes bright with male hostility. Clearly his blood was up. He made no effort to hide the fact he was disappointed with the turn of events.

"Probably twice as much as you." Mitch's swift change in demeanour instantly reminded the overseer who was boss. "Miss Reardon is as knowledgeable as any of us. She was reared on Wunnamurra. You might start to apologise."

Cody, keyed up, had not known exactly who Christine was, beyond one of the great Mitch Claydon's girlfriends. He immediately backed down, aware he had overstepped the mark. "Of course, I do apologize. I didn't realise, Miss Reardon."

Christine shrugged, said nothing, but Mitch spoke pointedly. "You didn't notice how she can ride?" He turned away pointedly. "So you're saying we give up on Lightning, Snowy?"

Snowy's perfect white teeth showed in a grimace. "I'm nervous about 'im, boss. He might break somebody's skull."

"He looks like he wants to do it now," Christine said uneasily, eyeing the haughty animal with a hollow chill. "He's impressive-looking, but there's something about his stare. There's a lot of violence in it."

Mitch ran a hand up over his golden-skinned face. "He's a wild horse. A tough, strong wild horse. But, yes, he does look a touch demented."

"Why don't you just let me rope him?" Jack Cody suggested, a veteran of more than a few rodeos. He tensed for rejection, thinking he could take the stallion whenever he wanted.

"I think you might finish up a casualty, Jack," Mitch said, knowing Cody had taken a bad fall at the last Darwin rodeo but unprepared to embarrass him.

"So this whole exercise has been a waste of time?" Cody couldn't contain his frustration. Who would have ever thought bigshot Claydon was a wimp?

"Him gotta bad spirit," Snowy observed, his long dark fingers stroking his chin.

Christine shot a quick look at the aboriginal elder, wondering whether Snowy was referring to Cody or the brumby. Maybe both.

"I reckon we don't want 'im boss. Good looker, but fulla vice. Let's look for the mares and foals. Pick 'em up."

The stallion was still displaying boldly, warning the riding party that this was his territory and to back off.

"If I can ride him home can I have him?" Cody let his tone match his inner bravado. "You know my reputation. I'm a really good rough rider."

"That horse could kill you, Jack," Mitch said. "He's never been handled. Now that we're seeing him up close, surely he looks unrideable to you, therefore valueless to the station. He won't make a good work horse after all, which was what this chase was all about."

Mitch provided the cool voice of reason, but Cody was as touchy as the stallion. His pride was on the line and he found himself wanting very badly indeed to impress the woman. She was beautiful and much more. Few would think to argue with Mitchell Claydon, but Cody wasn't entirely in control of himself—hadn't been from the first moment he'd laid eyes on Christine.

"He might surprise yah. Let me see if I can get a lasso over his head. I know as much about horses as any man on the station," Cody boasted, though it was far from the truth. Mitch was a superb horseman and Snowy was a renowned "breaker". "Horses have gotta respect humans," Cody said, alarming them all by suddenly producing a rope already noosed at one end. He rocked in the stirrups, then threw it while the rest of the party moved their mounts swiftly to the walls of the canyon.

"God Almighty!" Mitch was staggered by the overseer's actions, with so much potential danger for them all. "Back up further, Chris!" he yelled, his heart in his throat as he glimpsed her off to the right.

Incredibly the rope passed over the stallion's neck first time, but then all hell broke loose. The choking down process Cody had thought to accomplish to render the stallion either unconscious from lack of air or weak enough to fall to its knees, failed badly. The stallion was just too powerful. He objected violently to this ploy, thrashing his head from side to side in terror, eyes rolling whitely, so strong and heavily muscled Cody's horse was no match for it in the tussle. The station horse's sturdy legs were unable to sustain the weight of the stallion.

"Drop the rope, you bloody fool," Mitch shouted to Cody. "Get out of the way. That's an order."

But Cody, whose major fault was trying to impress women, was hell-bent on showing his skills. Not only that, he was terrified to let go in case the stallion—who was showing no sign of buckling, despite the noose being pulled tighter and tighter—bolted right at him in a mad panic to escape.

There was nothing for it, Mitch thought with cold fury, feeling his heart pound in reaction. Christine, his main concern, was offside, but there was no telling if the stallion would run straight at Cody or execute a series of maddened manoeuvres in his frenzy to escape. He couldn't begin to think of Christine hurt. Bloody, bruised and trampled. Cody, the arrogant bastard, had lost his senses.

Out of the corner of his eye Mitch saw Snowy too had his rope at the ready, waiting for the precise moment. Snowy never missed. Neither did he, but the stallion was as frightening an animal as Mitch had ever seen, and he'd seen plenty.

Even now he was kicking ferociously with both hind legs. If he didn't do something fast someone was going to get killed. As it was, the stallion looked as if he was going to smash right into the foolhardy Cody, or even attempt to go over him. Violence met with greater violence. It was obvious Cody couldn't cope. He was losing his nerve and his brave stockhorse was sliding further and further towards the lethal brumby.

The decision made, Mitch wasted little time. He found his rifle and dropped the stallion with a single shot, just at the critical moment. The sharp crack billowed out over the canyon, making the walls ring. The stallion's once powerful legs buckled under it as it fell dead to the sand.

Christine curled her arms around her body, her fists clenched so tightly her fingers seemed locked. Every one of them had faced the possibility of being injured, perhaps killed.

Cody, the cheeks of his narrow face turned concave, fell from the saddle, belly-flopping on the sand. "I just hope you realise what you did here this afternoon." Mitch stood over him, his voice deathly quiet when he really felt like raining blows on the fool. "I don't believe a man of your experience could be so incredibly stupid. What you did was criminal and against orders. The decision was to back off. You put us all at risk. What makes it more unforgivable is we have a woman with us."

Cody tried to sit up but flopped back, his legs shaking, his arms feeling as if they'd been pulled out of their sockets. Finally, with Claydon still standing over him, he stumbled to his feet, his hazel eyes mere slits in the sun. "I've never come across a brumby so strong or so savage," he defended himself, sounding shocked. "It's just not normal."

"You got that right!" Mitch said with some contempt. "What's not normal either is your lack of good sense. That horse could have killed someone on its way to freedom." Even so Mitch, like the others—all genuine horse-lovers, which Cody was not—found it distressing to see Lightning with his life snuffed out.

"You'd better ride back," Mitch told Cody curtly, wondering why the hell his father hadn't checked on this man's record. Why he himself hadn't either, for that matter, but they'd both trusted Leo Hendricks, Cody's late boss. "We all know about danger," he said through gritted teeth. "We face it time and again, but we have to exercise good judgement—not willingly and deliberately expose others to terrible trouble. That makes you a liability. How come Hendricks never said anything about that?"

"I've never been such a fool before." Cody pressed a hand to his swollen shoulder. He had very rapidly cooled down. Now he felt the rebuke like the sting of a whip.

He realized immediately he had lost his job. He had, in fact, been surprised when he'd got it. Hendricks's recommendation had been on the generous side. Worse would follow if he were fool enough to tangle with Mitch Claydon. The father was one thing; the son quite another. But he liked to think he might have an opportunity for revenge some time in the future. Claydon had made a fool of him in front of the woman, he thought bitterly. That struck him as unacceptable.

Still, he wasn't a complete fool. Cody pretended remorse. "Thanks, boss, you saved me." He looked directly at Claydon, feigning a humble look. "Apologizing won't do much good. What's done is done. But I'm left with the bad feeling I put you all at risk. Especially you, Miss Reardon.'' He touched the side of his wide-brimmed hat.

Christine nodded, but she had the odd sensation Cody wasn't feeling remorseful at all. As far as she was concerned there was something feral in that handsome narrow face.

CHAPTER FIVE

JULANNE was aghast at what might have happened. "You know what to do, Mitch. You have to sack him. That wasn't any kind of bravery; that was criminal stupidity."

Mitch looked out over the vast uninterrupted vistas from the homestead verandah, so used to his way of life he didn't often consider how privileged he was to own so much land. "How the heck did Dad hire him in the first place?" he queried, as if he didn't understand. He was sitting opposite his mother in one of the ten or more white wicker armchairs scattered along the front verandah, waiting for Christine to shower and change. He'd already washed up, but his mood was still edgy.

Julanne screwed up her face. "Well, Leo's a pal—some pal! But I had a feeling about Cody. He's strong and he's shown himself to be capable. He's always acted in a proper manner when he's come up to the house, but there's something about his eyes. There's no light in them."

"I didn't enjoy his reaction to Christine." Mitch bit down on his anger, his own sparkling gaze suddenly steely.

"In what way?" Julanne turned to stare at her son with open concern.

"He couldn't stop looking at her," Mitch said in a jaundiced tone. "But he was all innocence when I intercepted his stare."

Julanne visibly relaxed. "You can hardly blame him for looking, dear. Christine is simply stunning. Your own father admits he can't take his eyes off her."

Mitch downed his cold beer in one gulp. "That's entirely

different. Dad's watched Chris grow up. She could be another daughter. There's something in Cody's gaze that
might make a woman recoil. Chris is used to being stared
at, I know. I expect she didn't notice. But I sure as hell
did. Tasteless behaviour.''

"You still carry the torch," Julanne observed gently.

"I heard you, Mum."

Mitch still had the steam of anger coming off him,
Julanne thought, seeking to soothe. "The weekend is com-
ing up too quickly," she lamented. "Christine is due home
Sunday afternoon. Why don't I get a few people together
Saturday night?"

Mitch considered. "I don't know that Chris would want
that. Then again, she might. Who do you have in mind?"

Julanne turned her stately blonde head towards him.
"Kyall and Sarah, of course. And I suppose I should ask
Enid and Max?"

"No," Mitch said flatly, his eyes on a wedge-tailed eagle
soaring downwind. "Max is fine, but Enid could put quite
a dampener on the party. She's psychologically incapable
of not criticising Chris in some way."

"Tell me about it," Julanne invited dryly.

"If we're going to have a party, Chris has to enjoy herself."

"Of course, dear. So how do we go about leaving them
out?"

Mitch shrugged. "Keep everyone young. Unmarried or
soon to be married couples."

"That's you, I trust?" Julanne smiled at her adored son,
then gave his lean fingers a quick squeeze. "I can't wait
for you to marry and give your father and me grandchil-
dren."

"What's this?" Christine, stepping through the French
doors, pretended to prick up her ears. "I didn't even know

Mitch was engaged?'' This kind of banter she couldn't seem to stop.

"I have no head for engagements. I don't want to discuss them either.'' Mitch's tone was a velvet growl.

"Heavens, you sound grouchy!'' Christine came behind him, touched his cheek, then sank gracefully into the arm-chair beside him.

Soft fragrances wafted over him. Scents of shampoo, garlands of fresh flowers—Christine. "So do most men when they're getting pushed to the altar,'' he drawled.

"You'd probably make a totally lousy husband anyway.'' Christine reached out a hand and tousled his thick golden hair, not satisfied until it flopped boyishly onto his forehead.

"I've got a notion you'd make a very dangerous wife.'' He smoothed his hair.

"How's that?'' Her sapphire eyes were alive with mischief.

"A man would have to lock you up. Beautiful women are the most problematic of all. That's why so many guys marry plain women. Did you happen to notice the way Cody was looking at you?''

Christine sat back, as fresh and cool in her lacy white camisole top and matching skirt as the white daisies that surrounded them in glazed pots. Her long lustrous mane of hair framed her face and trailed down her back; her skin was peachy and glowing from the sun. He felt free to indulge his searing desire to look at her, store up his memories before she went back to the world she had made for herself.

"Actually, I did,'' she confessed. "I've encountered looks like that many times before, both professionally and socially. I love you for being jealous, Mitch.''

He had to deal with that. ''Except I'd have felt the same way for any woman guest.''

''Ouch!''

''You deserved that.''

''I know,'' she said ruefully, wanting to draw some response from him in any way she could. ''What's wrong with you anyway? I know you're angry about the whole thing. Are you mad that you have to sack him?''

''No problem.'' He shrugged. A little trickle of water was running from a lock of her damp hair down her neck and into the cleft of her breasts. He had to wrestle with the insane urge to lap it with his tongue. Instead he continued casually. ''Except I have to pay Dad the courtesy of clearing it with him. Dad, as you know, is staying overnight in town. He really enjoys his card evenings with the boys. You'd better tell Chris what you plan for her, Mum.''

''What's this?'' Christine turned fully Julanne's way.

''How would you like a party Saturday night?'' Julanne asked. ''Just young people. No oldies. You and Mitch, Sarah and Kyall…''

''I think we should make up a list. That's if Chris wants a party.''

''Why wouldn't I want a party, Mitch?'' She raised her arched brows at him. ''That's a lovely idea, Julanne. I'm thinking we could ask some of Mitch's old girlfriends. There's Fleur McPherson—''

''Turns out she's married.'' Mitch balanced on two legs of his turquoise and white upholstered chair.

''Is she really? I didn't know that.'' Christine looked at him in surprise.

''Think how long you've been away,'' he retorted acidly.

''Fancy that—Fleur married!'' She had always liked Fleur, though they had never been that close. End of story, then. We can't break that up.''

"Have your fun," he invited.

"I'm an old girlfriend too," she pointed out.

"Only you're out of my system."

"That's truly sad."

"You screwed up."

"We're talking about a party, children." Julanne tapped the glass-topped table.

"I don't want to make a lot of work for you," Christine said, knowing how Julanne went to endless trouble. "We should keep the numbers down."

"We'll only invite the ones you really like," Mitch suggested. "But we'll have to let them know as soon as possible so they can make arrangements."

"Let's make the list, then,' Julanne said, loving the whole idea. "If we keep it to, say, between twenty and thirty, we can accommodate everyone overnight."

"But what do I do for a party dress?" a pleasantly surprised Christine asked.

"You brought one with you, surely?" Mitch shot her a mocking glance, at the same time considering the magic of Christine in a party dress.

"Not with me, no." Then, as she further pondered, "You mean here to Marjimba?"

"I mean in amongst all the luggage you brought home to Wunnamurra," Mitch corrected with sarcasm. "If you didn't live way out here you'd have been mobbed already. Christine Reardon, superstar."

"The fact I'm not a star out here is a great big plus, I can tell you: I'm not enthralled by having my bottom pinched black and blue. Some of them are even schoolboys. They sort of follow you in packs."

"In Australia?" Mitch sounded so horrified she might have been speaking of violent offenders.

"I have to say mostly in Italy, where they're much more

enthusiastic about women. Or this woman, though I'm sensible enough to know looks are transient—like my so-called fame. Now, as luck would have it, I did bring a couple of glamorous dresses with me. For all I knew Mother might have been desperate to give me a party."

"I suppose there are no words to describe them?" Mitch asked. Image after image of Christine in and out of dresses ran through his mind as if they were being played on a video camera. It was a stimulus Mitch tried hard to suppress, though Christine was looking at him with such a sweet mocking smile she might have been reading his mind.

"Sorry, Mitch! You'll just have to wait and see. I tell you who I would like to see after all this time—Shelley Logan. She was such a sweet little kid. A real pixie. But she must be all grown up by now?"

"She's still petite." Julanne smiled. "Personally, I think she looks like an adorable little witch. I know she had a twenty-first birthday not that long ago. She didn't get a party. Her parents treated her by giving her a day off work."

"That's a bit of an exaggeration, Mum," Mitch said, effortlessly maintaining his balance on the two legs of his chair.

"Not much. They brought her into town for lunch. The parties are kept for Amanda. Shelley must be terribly hurt the way her mother and father favour her older sister."

"You mean they broke her heart," Christine replied without hesitation. They all knew the story of the Logans. "Shelley was punished for surviving when her twin, Sean, didn't." Sean had been the boy and Pat Logan's pride and joy. "That was a tragedy."

"It had a dreadful impact on the family." Julanne looked sad. "Little Shelley took the blame for her big sister. The twins were six. Amanda was eleven. She should never have taken them down to the creek.''

"I always had it in my mind that Amanda wandered off and left them,'' Christine said. "But she told a different story. One that made Shelley out to be a very naughty, disobedient little girl. That wasn't the way I saw it. Shelley was such a cute little thing—bright as a button, red hair on fire and the most beautiful big green eyes. I remember her as being quite motherly with Sean. It was lovely to see.''

"Then he died.'' Julanne sighed sadly, and tender-hearted Christine momentarily closed her eyes. "Drowned. I suppose we'll never know the truth of it,'' she reflected. "They still work the property, but Pat's heart went out of it when he lost his boy. They were really struggling until Shelley got the bright idea to take in tourists.''

"Really? When did this happen?'' Christine enquired.

"A year or so ago. It's an 'Outback Encounter' kind of trip. The station hosts a small party of guests at a time. It gives tourists a taste of the real Australia. Shelley's really very clever. But the family work her too hard. She does all the cooking, organizes the activities, while Amanda sits around in the evening looking pretty. It's not cheap, but the meals are excellent, the accommodation is comfortable, and Shelley works very hard to make the trip memorable. They're never short of visitors. They attract Europeans and Japanese mostly.''

"Taking in tourists is keeping their heads above water,'' Mitch remarked. "All due to Shelley, though she doesn't get much praise for herself from dear Daddy, no matter how hard she tries. If you want to invite Shelley, and I think you should, you'll have to invite Amanda as well, otherwise they'll all give Shelley hell.''

"So things don't change?'' Christine mused, shaking back her drying mane.

"Not with the Logans. The family was destroyed by Sean's death and Shelley was sadly made the scapegoat."

In the end they made a list of twenty young people who would fit in perfectly. The numbers included quite a few of Mitch's polo pals, a fact Christine commented on.

"It's a way of life out here," he pointed out, as though that guaranteed their invitation to the party. "You of all people shouldn't object, Chris. You used to love watching the game."

"And that's what I had to do. Watch. I wanted to play."

"You were such a daredevil you'd have been hurt."

"And you weren't?" Her eyes flew to his in challenge.

"The sport is too dangerous for a woman, Chrissy. I couldn't have borne to be around had something happened to you."

Her eyes, incredibly, stung with tears. She looked down, blinking them away. "You can't imagine how that comforts me. Now, who's this? Tony Norman?" She took refuge in consulting the list.

"You'll like him." Julanne patted her arm. "He's the overseer on Strathmore. Very likeable and good fun."

"My life has changed so much. I haven't kept up with anybody." Christine lamented.

"Yeah, well, we all know that." Mitch's voice was bone-dry. "But everyone will be very curious to see you."

"We'd better get cracking, then!" Christine sprang up with enthusiasm. Her own mother hadn't suggested a party but Julanne had. "I want you to know I love you, Julanne." Affectionately she dropped a kiss on Julanne's head, before disappearing through the open French doors into the house.

"I tell you what you have to do, my darling," Julanne said broodingly to her son. "You have to win that girl back."

Mitch's attractive voice rasped. "How sorry do you want

me to be the next time, Mum?'' He rose restlessly, shoving back his chair before moving to the white wrought-iron balustrade where he stared fixedly at the landscape. The sheer incandescence of it!

''In no time at all Chris will want to return to her glamorous world—the Manhattan apartment, the soap star, being famous.'' He turned back to his mother, as though reminding her. ''She's no ordinary woman. She's a supermodel. Look at her! God, the polish she's acquired! She's been working at it for years. I don't know about schoolboys, but most men's mouths would fall open when they see her pass by. She's got such flash all around her. So don't get up any false hopes. I couldn't go through it again. I'm happy enough just the way I am. Free from emotional pain.''

Even as he said it he thought that one night alone with Christine would be worth all the agony. His body was crying out for her. Having her in his home, right under his nose, was both heaven and hell. Just how much punishment was a man supposed to take?

He hadn't learned a darn thing.

It was wonderful when they all came together—the friends Christine had left behind, laughing and joking, reminiscing about the life they had shared, the childhood friendships that had been so strong. Everyone was relaxed and comfortable from the moment they arrived, secure in the knowledge that they could party all night if they wanted to because they were all staying over. The girls were to be accommodated at the homestead, while the young men could find a bunk at the staff quarters.

Ten couples in all had been invited, so Julanne had decided on a sit-down dinner rather than a buffet. The antique oak table in the formal dining room could seat twenty-four when fully extended, and Julanne, a born hostess, with too few occasions to go to town on entertaining, loved to use it.

Kyall and Sarah, looking simply beautiful in an ice-blue sequinned slip dress, arrived first, flying in with other guests they had picked up *en route*. Among them were the Logan girls, Amanda and Shelley, and the Saunders brothers, who were members of Kyall's polo team, as was Mitch. The McIvor girls, in sparkling form, arrived by helicopter, as did Terry and Alex Cooper. The rest made the trip overland, arriving in T-shirts and jeans and making the transition to party gear hours later. Everyone came to see their home-grown superstar, Christine, and to have fun.

Christine didn't disappoint. She wore a dream of a dress that produced appreciative oohs and aahs and shrieks of laughter as she gave an over-the-top catwalk demonstration. Made of layers of floaty whisper-weight silk chiffon, the dress was patterned in floral swirls of pink and violet, blue and lime-green. The long, softly tiered skirt was asymmetrical, falling from knee height to the ankle, the neckline of the slip top dipped deep, and her high-heeled gold sandals showed off her lovely feet and legs.

"A marvellous dress for the heat." Amanda Logan, who had lots of fantasies revolving around the extremely hard-to-get Mitch Claydon, tossed her blonde head challengingly, thinking that the dress must have cost a couple of thousand dollars at least. She'd been well pleased with the way she looked—decidedly sexy—until she caught sight of Christine. She was stunning, of course—Amanda had seen all the pictures in the magazines—but much too tall. And why she would want to wear stiletto heels was a mystery!

"Or alternatively she could start a heatwave of her own." Mitch cut in on Amanda, sparkling eyes sweeping over Christine in a way Amanda definitely didn't like.

''That's some dress!'' he told Christine, not bothering to hide his male appreciation. ''I don't think you should ever take it off.''

Julanne looking into her huge living room, embraced the colourful scene. Everyone looked happy. All the young women—she had known them from childhood—had gone to a good deal of trouble to look their best. Their dresses were very pretty. Julanne loved the romantic look currently in vogue—it was just the thing for a summer party.

Amanda's was perhaps a touch too provocative—a scarlet mini-dress fringed with beads and revealing a little too much creamy bosom. Amanda was a very pretty young woman—though she didn't have a tenth of Shelley's character—and Julanne was perfectly well aware she had had her sights set on Mitch for some time. She'd already given him a very showy kiss when she'd arrived.

The young men, all friends of Mitch and Kyall, were considerably smartened up from their everyday uniform of denim shirts and jeans. They wore soft summer-weight suits with trendy dress shirts and silk-woven ties.

Dinner went off perfectly. Julanne, helped by Noni, their housekeeper, had a lot of fun serving up the delicious menu they had worked out: a banquet of fresh seafood flown in especially for the party from the tropical north of the state. They all dined regularly on the best of station beef, lamb, pork, veal and game, but seafood wasn't readily available on the desert fringe. Consequently all the compliments that were forthcoming had Julanne flushed with pleasure.

There were oysters in champagne sauce, stir-fried crab cream, magnificent ocean prawns served with a sauce of Indian spices, sea scallops wrapped with grilled bacon and served with a red wine sauce, and as a centrepiece superb Red Emperors—one of the great eating fish of the world—

steamed in banana leaves with papaya chilli and coconut salsa.

Afterwards, for anyone who could fit it in, there was dessert of either passion fruit and citrus salad sorbet, or peppered pineapple with vanilla ice cream. Everyone, with the exception of three of the girls who complained pleasurably that they would have to go on a diet for a week, fell on the offer.

"How do you manage to eat so much and stay so slim?" Amanda asked Christine, looking thoroughly bewildered. Amanda, who wasn't a great one for exercise, tended to put on weight easily.

"One of the pluses of being tall." Christine threw Amanda a smile, aware she had been observing her closely all evening. "But I do watch my diet and I work out. This is a very special occasion. It's a lovely banquet and everything tastes so good!" Christine grasped Julanne's arm as she was passing. "Thank you so much, Julanne. You're so good to me. I'll never forget."

"Didn't I hold you when you were a baby?" Julanne answered, looking well pleased. "Kyall too." Julanne smiled fondly at Christine's brother and his beautiful fiancée Sarah beside him.

"My mind flies back to the time Mitch and Chris, Sarah and I thought it would be wonderful to find the 'Claydon Treasure'," Kyall said, putting his hand over Sarah's. "We all got lost following some old map Mitch offered as proof of the treasure's existence."

"I remember that as if it were yesterday." Mitch smiled, his tanned face and golden hair seeming to attract all the light. "There *is* a treasure. No joke. Mum, why don't you sit down and tell us about it?" he begged.

"I'm sure most of you know."

"Please, Julanne," Christine urged. "Even I don't know the whole story."

"I don't know it at all," Shelley Logan joined in.

"Heavens, you were a toddler when they went on that search," her sister reminded her tartly. "Darling Sean was still alive."

Shelley's expression went from vivid to stricken, and the whole table—with the exception of her own sister—seemed to gather around her.

Christine smiled in empathy at this young woman who'd had to cope with that sort of thing for most of her life. Shelley looked so fragile—she was a petite five foot three—but from all accounts she was the rock of the Logan family. Christine, the experienced fashion model, realised that with very little effort Shelley, with her porcelain skin, big green eyes and explosive mop of red-gold curls, could be made to look quite beautiful. But it was Amanda's saucy red dress and red satin slingbacks that had cost the money, not Shelley's pretty outfit that made her look like a teenager. There was something about Shelley Logan that tugged at the heartstrings.

Pressed on all sides, Julanne sat down, launching into the tale of the Claydon "Treasure".

"We're going back to the 1840s now, when Edward Claydon, a well-to-do native of England, his wife Cornelia and his young family of two sons and two daughters took up a great selection of some three hundred thousand acres on the fertile tablelands of the Darling Downs—which, as you know, is some one hundred and sixty kilometres west of Brisbane.

"These days the Darling Downs are known as the granary of Queensland, but in the early days settlers like the Claydons raised sheep, which they drove overland from the Hunter Valley in New South Wales. It was Edward

Claydon's intention, like many another adventurer who made the long dangerous sea trip, to come to this country and establish his own dynasty. And when there was a serious outbreak of disease among sheep in those early years he undertook to move himself, his family and his healthy flock of ten thousand sheep and one thousand cattle much farther on. Here to Marjimba, in fact, which was about as far away as he could get.

"Here he settled. Here he prospered, with no threats from the aboriginal people on his vast selection. The threat came instead in the form of a bushranger called Paddy Balfour, an escaped convict servant who took over a twenty-man gang called 'Balfour's Bunch' and spent a number of years—until he had the brains to quit—roaming the bush.

"The gang's main target was new South Wales, but as the reward on his head kept increasing Balfour and his bunch headed for South-West Queensland. They held up quite a few settlers living in isolation, so Edward Claydon decided to get together all the gold he possessed, as well as his wife's jewellery—most of it inherited from her rich merchant-class English family—and hide it from Balfour and his criminal bunch. The only trouble was Edward neglected to tell anyone where he buried the treasure.

"His fears about being robbed by the gang, though understandable, were never realised. The gang broke up after two of the party were shot dead by the terrified wife of a small settler who had been left alone while her husband was away droving. At almost the same time Edward was killed by a horse thief who returned his fire. When the family began to recover from their sudden violent loss they started to wonder about the treasure."

"And they've been wondering to this day," Mitch said, looking very handsome and relaxed.

"And the map?" Shelley's green eyes were huge.

"It took us two miles away from the homestead before we were forced by heat and weariness to abandon the adventure." Mitch smiled. "Chrissy couldn't keep up."

"That's not the way I remember it." Christine's eyes touched his in mock challenge. "I could keep up with you, Mitch Claydon, any time. How old were we, Sarah?"

"You were the youngest, at nine." Sarah smiled. "Kyall—" she touched his arm with rich contentment "—was eleven, going on twelve. Mitch and I came in between. I know we all got into a lot of trouble. You especially, Chris," she added with a tiny grimace, remembering the wretched consequences of their adventure.

"Isn't that the truth?" Mitch's tone was crisp. He hadn't forgotten either, though a lot of time had gone by. The youngest member of the party Christine, the least responsible, had endured a tongue-lashing at home. Not so Kyall. Never Kyall. Though he had always sprung instantly to his sister's defence.

"So no one in the family has the slightest clue as to where Edward hid the treasure?" Shelley asked, restoring him to the present. "Surely it could have been somewhere in the house? A secret place?"

"Do you think we haven't looked?" Mitch gave her a comical look. "Over the years Chris and I searched every nook and cranny." And made love while we were at it, he thought, watching colour creep up into Christine's beautiful skin. "The treasure is nowhere to be found."

"But where did the map come from?" Shelley was fascinated. What a difference a "treasure" would make to her struggling family.

"I think it was just a bit of fun." Mitch had long since concluded this. "The map was folded very small and stuck into a toy stagecoach. Not a toy, really, now a collectable.

The Harlequin Reader Service® — Here's how it works:

Accepting your 2 free books and mystery gift places you under no obligation to buy anything. You may keep the books and gift and return the shipping statement marked "cancel." If you do not cancel, about a month later we'll send you 6 additional books and bill you just $3.34 each in the U.S., or $3.80 each in Canada, plus 25¢ shipping and handling per book and applicable taxes if any.* That's the complete price and — compared to cover prices of $3.99 in the U.S. and $4.50 in Canada — it's quite a bargain! You may cancel at any time, but if you choose to continue, every month we'll send you 6 more books, which you may either purchase at the discount price or return to us and cancel your subscription.

*Terms and prices subject to change without notice. Sales tax applicable in N.Y. Canadian residents will be charged applicable provincial taxes and GST. Credit or debit balances in a customer's account(s) may be offset by any other outstanding balance owed by or to the customer.

Play the *Lucky Hearts* Game

and get...

2 FREE BOOKS
and a FREE MYSTERY GIFT...
Yes! YOURS to KEEP!

I have scratched off the silver card. Please send me my *2 FREE BOOKS* and *FREE mystery GIFT*. I understand that I am under no obligation to purchase any books as explained on the back of this card.

Scratch Here!
then look below to see what your cards get you... 2 Free Books & a Free Mystery Gift!

386 HDL DU6V   **186 HDL DU7D**

FIRST NAME   LAST NAME

ADDRESS

APT.#   CITY

STATE/PROV.   ZIP/POSTAL CODE   (H-RA-08/03)

Twenty-one gets you
2 FREE BOOKS
and a *FREE MYSTERY GIFT!*

Twenty gets you
2 FREE BOOKS!

Nineteen gets you
1 FREE BOOK!

TRY AGAIN!

Offer limited to one per household and not valid to current Harlequin Romance® subscribers. All orders subject to approval.

It was made late eighteenth century. It's still there, in one of those cupboards.'' He indicated a long wall of built-in cabinets just behind him, the upper sections glass-fronted, displaying a collection of beautiful porcelain—plates, dishes, tureens, vases and numerous figurines—along with a fine collection of silverware.

"Show it to her, Mitch." Christine looked at him, sparkling-eyed. "This is all part of the legend."

"Will do, ma'am." Mitch stood up and executed a flourishing bow in Christine's direction. He walked to the long line of cabinets and a moment later returned to the dining table with the toy stagecoach, which he placed on the table in front of Shelley.

"Oh, isn't that sweet?"

"Valuable too," Mitch told her. "A collector's item. Quite rare."

Shelley touched the wooden coach with a reverent finger. There was a little curtain at the window, four pieces of luggage on top, the driver up front, a man riding shotgun to the rear. Both wore brown cloth overcoats with long black hats. "And the map's still inside?"

"Let her see it, Mitch," Christine prompted, thinking how different Shelley was from her sister. Amanda wasn't looking at all pleased to see Shelley enjoying this special attention.

"Okay." Mitch's lean strong fingers worked delicately and he opened the coach door, withdrawing a slip of yellowed paper.

"What about making some copies?" Christine joked.

"Yeah, what do you say, Mitch?" Rick Saunders grinned. "Could be a spotter's fee?"

"I can safely say there would be a handsome reward for anyone who could find it. But needless to say the treasure belongs to the Claydons. Damn, where is it?"

"Deep in the desert," Christine said. "All of you are free to start digging." She looked around the table at the laughing guests.

Shelley studied the map in her hand.

"Can you spot a clue?" What a miracle that would be, if the "Claydon Treasure" was ever found. Christine leaned forward. She and Mitch had hovered over it endlessly in the old days, Mitch all the while stopping to steal kisses from her mouth.

"One," Shelley said.

That drew a chorus of "Wha-a-t?" from all four early treasure-hunters—Mitch, Christine, Kyall and Sarah.

"I suppose it's the one you all saw?" Shelley broke off to raise her eyes playfully.

Mitch eased back into his chair. "Whisper it, Shelley, right now."

"Hell, I'm getting excited," Kyall only half joked, watching Shelley cup her hand around her mouth and whisper into Mitch's ear.

Mitch leaned back and stared at her as if at a distant horizon. "None of us saw what you saw, Shelley," he said finally.

"Which is what?" Christine held out her hand for the map. "Come on, Mitch. We need to know and that's a fact."

"This is top secret, I assure you, dearest Chrissy. I'd better keep it to myself."

"I'll get it out of you," she said, and signals like flashes of lightning were going from one to the other.

The others laughed and looked Shelley's way. "Right, now we're counting on you to tell us, Shel," Rick Saunders, who was more than half in love with Shelley Logan, urged.

"I'm not going to say a word about it to anyone. Not

anyone!'' Shelley gave her wide entrancing smile. "When Mitch turns up the family fortune I'm the one who's going to get the spotter's fee, not you, Rick.''

It was a prediction to be played out in the fullness of time. For that evening, with its wonderful relaxed atmosphere, Christine only thought of it as a highly improbable but perfect solution. If she helped find the treasure, then maybe Shelley Logan wouldn't have to work quite so hard for her family.

CHAPTER SIX

"DANCE with me," Mitch said, determinedly waving off one of the Cooper brothers and drawing Christine into his arms.

This was the first time he'd been able to get to her since the dance music had started up well over an hour ago. All of the guys had wanted to dance with her, no doubt so they could boast about it later. If the truth were known he was starting to get fed up with all the clowning around, but it was obvious Christine was enjoying herself. That was what the party was all about after all. She couldn't help being so beautiful, so warm, so friendly.

He tipped his head back a little, to survey her. The world reduced to just one woman. "How's it going?"

A breathless girl stumbled as she almost backed into them. With a ripple of laughter and apology she and her partner moved off. Mitch seized the opportunity to catch Christine tightly around her slender waist and twirl her further down the floodlit terrace. He vividly remembered all the Outback dances they had attended together. Music pouring out of bush bands, washing over them, the hot blood in their veins, the nimble feet. He and Chris had been so good at dancing together they'd given impromptu exhibitions.

"I'm loving every minute," she responded, all her senses leaping from the fire that burned bright in her.

Just to be back in his arms was heaven. How she'd longed for him to come to her. Willed it. No minutes were more precious than those with Mitch. Why didn't she tell him that? Surely she could get through to him? Couldn't he read the expression in her eyes? He'd been wearing Amanda Logan on his arm all night like some sort of protective wing. But if he expected her to be jealous he was going to be disappointed.

"I've been dying to ask. What did Shelley see that we didn't?" Surprise had been written all over his face. It had intrigued her.

"No way I'm going to tell you." His smile was slow and teasing.

She searched his face, his golden hair like a halo, his mouth curved in a half-smile. "I'll worry about it all night."

"So will I. If I ever get the time I'll follow it up. I might even ask you along."

"Are you serious?" She stared at him incredulously.

He shook his head. "Hell, it's the same old map. It's been circulating for more than one hundred and fifty years. Shelley saw one thing we might have missed, though there's very probably nothing in it."

"Great—and you won't tell me? You simply have no idea how I'll fret."

"Why don't you come and share my bed with me? We could talk about it there. For a while."

Her heart literally shook. It moved halfway up her throat. "All right, I'll play this stupid game."

"No game."

"It's what you want?" she asked carefully.

"It could be a great idea." He utilized the mocking tone he had developed like armour against her.

"You could be lying."

He closed his fingers around her blue-veined wrist. "Lies complicate an already complicated existence."

"Why do we do it then?"

"Why do I do it with you, you mean?" He smiled at her but the mockery didn't stop. "Self-protection, Christine. If you don't love, you don't lose. Losing can be horribly wounding."

"Somehow we've got to work through this, Mitch."

"Why?" Marshal your defences, he reminded himself. Line up your arguments before you answer. She can knock them down in less than a minute.

"Because it's important. For all that's happened, we still care about each other."

"You mean I want you," he corrected bluntly. "What I feel now is lust, not love. Wanting isn't always the right thing to do, but I'm afraid that's a matter beyond repair. The flesh has a life of its own."

"Let's start with your head," she challenged.

He hauled her closer, their bodies moving in the old way, rhythmically, in perfect unison. "My head rejects you."

"That's terribly sad."

"Isn't it? Come here." He said it as though she was about to break away. "It doesn't stop either of us functioning. I carry much of the responsibility for the station now. You've made a big success of yourself. So we're both performing more than adequately, despite our little estrangement."

"I don't feel estranged." She felt inflamed. Madly, hotly yearning, desirous. Heart slumbrous, body light as thistledown in his arms.

"How do you feel?" he asked.

"Awfully in love with you. It's as though my heart's set in concrete."

For a moment he almost lost it. "Ah, stop it," he chided, grinding her beautiful, slender body against him in ecstasy and a kind of rage.

"You asked the question. I answered."

"You're trying to re-establish yourself in my life?"

She could have recoiled from his blazing eyes. Instead she let her breath surge, then subside. "If you'll let me in."

He swallowed hard on a stifled groan, feeling inadequate to the task of pushing this woman away. This woman who made all his senses run riot.

"What then?" he demanded. "We get back to the same situation. You'll decide again you really shouldn't have made any commitment. We have to let go, Chris. You no longer fit in here."

That hurt terribly. "You didn't used to be cruel," she whispered, swaying in his arms.

"You can take the blame for that. Cruelty is a way of maintaining distance."

"So you're never going to forgive me?"

It was all he could do not to pick her up and carry her off with violence and passion. "It's not a question of forgiveness," he said bluntly. "I fear being in love with you, Chrissy. There. I've admitted it. I fear all the rage, the loneliness and frustration. Losing you was too painful an experience to want to chance it again."

"Yet you want to go to bed with me?"

He relaxed his firm hold on her. "Should that be a surprise? You're a very beautiful, experienced woman. Sex doesn't always end in disaster. Love can—and does."

"So you're prepared to forfeit love for the likes of Amanda Logan? I couldn't help seeing her wrapped around your arm."

He didn't respond immediately, aware he was guilty of allowing Amanda to cling. "Surely you're not jealous? There's no need to be."

"You're giving Amanda encouragement. I'm not jealous, as it so happens. I just don't think it's a good idea."

''You're absolutely right about that. Amanda's too ready to leap into my arms.''

''She should play harder to get.''

''Chrissy, darling, don't interfere. You're out of my life, remember?''

''How could I forget, when you keep telling me? There's no hope I could get back?'' Her sapphire eyes implored; she was breathless with the effort.

''Why are you doing this?'' He bent his head over hers, such a terrible rending sensation inside him. ''In no time at all you'll be out of here. The vacation will be over. You'll have to move on. Make yet another escape. It can't have been all that easy to move to the top of your profession anyway.''

''Strangely enough, it was. That's the irony of it. My agency called my rise 'meteoric'. I was lucky. I had the right look at the right time.''

''And the celebrities of the fashion world are your friends. You've spent your time winging around the great capitals of the world. Even your family couldn't keep track of you. You're used to million-dollar contracts, nightclubs, dinner parties, gala functions—the high life. Hell, you must have brushed up against some wild people—the drug scene, even. Modelling must expose you to all sorts.''

She drew back in surprise. Somehow she'd thought he would never touch on that subject. He knew her, the sort of person she was. ''Sure I have,'' she freely admitted, ''but that scene scares me to death. I hate it mostly for the ones who seem powerless to stop themselves from entering it. I don't do drugs, Mitch. Never have, never will. It's outside my code. I'm not promiscuous either.''

''God, did I say you were?'' The very thought of her in nameless men's arms shocked him to the core. This was the woman who had once been everything to him. Who still made him come sensually alive.

"I think in your head you've exaggerated my way of life," Christine said quietly. "You've probably heard too much about fashion identities hooked on alcohol or drugs. I keep my feet on the ground. I may have changed on the surface, but I'm the same person underneath."

"I'm supposed to believe that, Chrissy?" he asked. "You're surely not trying to tell me you're ready to give it all up? Come home?"

She looked across the brightly lit terrace and saw Amanda staring their way, her pretty face pinched in envy. "I'll have to eventually. I'd say I have a couple more years at the outside. Youth is the name of the modelling game. Adorable little twelve-year-olds all made up to achieve the look. Starving themselves into the bargain. It's a serious problem. Still, they're making the pages."

"So there's life after modelling?" He sounded highly sceptical.

"It's about time I lived it." Trembling in his embrace, she allowed her hand to caress the back of his neck, compulsively smoothing it.

"Stop that!" He spoke with deceptive gentleness. What a rare gift she had for raising passion's ecstasy.

"Scaredy-cat!" she whispered beneath her breath, just like when they were children. His hair was like thick silk, his skin beneath the hair velvet.

"Turns out I am," he answered with a kind of deep self-disgust. "Some part of me will always be mad about you, Chrissy, but not mad enough. So stop all the little tricks. Where exactly would you live? It wouldn't be all that easy falling off centre stage. The glory and the adulation over."

"None of it was in demand from me. I don't need adulation. As I said, my feet are on the ground. I don't have stars in my eyes, Mitch. Being a well-known model isn't the sole object of my life. It was an avenue that gave me worldly success and a lot of pleasure, but I think I can survive the loss.''

"And what if you're mistaken?'' His gaze was searching.

"You'll never trust me again, so why answer? That terrible thought nags at me.''

"As well it might,'' he confirmed dryly. "I can only tell you this, Chrissy. I'm not about to have my heart ripped out twice.'' Even as he said it, perversely he pulled her closer, roused and arousing. Electric currents passed from his body to hers, spreading through every fibre, every nerve. It was a fever that would endure.

That was his brain talking, of course. The only problem was his body wasn't listening. The pleasure of holding Christine so intimately in his arms was rapture. It was damned nearly killing him. He wanted her...craved her...from the depths of his clamouring heart. He wanted to cover her with kisses, let his hand shape her breasts, move down over her body. He did let one hand slip to her hip-bone, moving his knee between her long lovely legs in a contrived movement of the dance. Hunger was sweeping over him like veils of sand in a dust storm. Not another woman in the world could deliver him such pleasure. Christine as a lover had never been surpassed.

In the shelter of a lush springing palm, desire peaked. He abandoned all pretence, scooping her beautiful face into his hands, placing his mouth where it most urgently wanted to be.

Was there a split second's resistance or sizzling shock? Whatever, he couldn't control the pressure, increasing it, wanting more and more, while her lips opened like a flower, so perfect for his loving, her tongue the stamen, circling his with tiny little darting flickers. It flooded him with passion, urging him on.

Her eyes were closed. He could feel the tickle of her long eyelashes. Somehow she had melted into him in the most ravishing fusion, her body hot beneath the flimsy silk-chiffon. He wanted to say, Come away with me. He wanted to take her hand, guide her back through the house to his sanctuary of the west wing. He wanted the unparalleled sensation of undressing her.

The very thought filled his blood with sparks. He thought his strong hands must be crushing her satiny cheeks, but she didn't complain. Not a whimper. If anything she was letting his mouth devour her in an effort to drive away the anguish. He'd told himself over and over he couldn't put himself through any more, yet here he was, control gone, mortified by desire.

Kissing wasn't enough. It had never been enough. He had to know that body, so perfectly constructed for his loving. He wanted her naked in his bed, between his sheets. He wanted to stretch the length of his hard sinewy body beside her. He wanted to drive his manhood deep, deep into her.

Ecstasy!

He loved her. It was a force of habit. Though that love was full of desperation. Once they had been the most likely couple in the world. That they were going to get married a foregone conclusion. Now they were the most unlikely pair. She was expelled from his life. The cattleman and the fashion model. Her career, her dramatic rise to the heights, had wrecked all his dreams. There had to be more for him than memories.

With a muffled, feeling-charged exclamation he released her, inhaling the scent of her on him, breathing it in like oxygen, staring down into her beautiful impassioned face, the desperate wide eyes.

"That was stupid." His voice turned sober, cracked with tension. "In fact madness."

She confronted him with rising agitation. With love and longing for this hot-hearted, hard-headed man. "What's wrong with you, Mitch? Do you like it this way? Loving me, hating me?"

To admit to it was unthinkable. "What I'd love is to take you in a way you'd never forget. I wouldn't let you out of my room for days, maybe weeks."

"Only you lack the courage to try it. You cherish your old grief, Mitch. You nurse it along. I betrayed you. You don't let me ever forget it. Everything or nothing." She held a hand over her racing heart. It didn't beat like this even after a strenuous workout. "You're wallowing in self-pity," she accused him. "Is it so utterly impossible to pity me? Yes, and I'll tell you why. You let your pride choke you."

"Really?" Anger ran through him like a dark, bitter undercurrent. It showed itself in the blue flash of his eyes, the set of his head and shoulders, the force of his grip. "Even now you're trying to control me. You know it. You want to stay the only woman who has gone deep down inside me. Some women are like that."

"Not me!" She seemed to be straining to breathe.

"You can't take rejection, Chrissy, any more than I could. I loved you," he said fiercely, "but you didn't care enough. This is all about power now. The power of a beautiful woman. You're used to making a spectacular impact. It probably keeps you sparking on all cylinders. Only you're not asserting that power over me. I'm tired of wasting my life over you. It's agonizing. I'm the fool who's lived a stupid dream. It's kept me from getting on with my life. But the world wouldn't end if you left me again. I've survived separation once already.''

''I have too. Don't you think the knowledge I hurt you so badly bites deep? I'm so sorry. I'm beseeching you to sweep away the unhappy past.''

''It's not that easy, Chrissy.'' He shook his head.

''Let it rest!''

''It's hard to forget what you did.''

''Then why do you kiss me like you do?'' She locked her eyes on his face. ''It makes no sense.''

''I'm human,'' he gritted. ''Sometimes it's impossible for me to understand myself. Pride means everything to a man.''

''What's pride got to do with it when we're talking about love?''

''Who said I still love you?'' Behind his head was the dazzling star-studded sky.

''I say you do.''

''No more.'' He shook his head. ''The answer's simple. It's sex, Chrissy. I'll say again, sex has nothing to do with love or happiness.''

''Agreed—only I don't accept what you're saying. You're trying to punish me. I know you, Mitch. We grew up together, remember? You loved me as your friend before we ever became lovers.''

''A profound mistake.'' His tone was dark. ''I've relinquished faith in you, Chrissy, when once I had all the faith in the world. For all I know you could be looking for great sex too. Despite everything we know it'd still work.''

''Except I don't come cheap.''

''That goes without saying. So what do you want? It can't be money. I think it's still possession.''

Shadowed by the palm, blind and deaf to everything but themselves and their abandonment to anger, they failed to hear a sweet syrupy voice until the owner of the voice was almost upon them.

"Mitch, where are you?" It was Amanda, pretending she didn't know where Mitch had disappeared to when she'd been keeping him and Christine under close surveillance all night.

"Damn!" Mitch sobered in an instant. "You never know what to expect with Amanda."

"I'd call it an ambush." Christine tossed her hair back from her heated face. "You go and pay her a lot of attention, Mitch. It'll take your mind off me and hopefully dull your senses. I'll go back the other way." With that she moved with the swiftness of a gazelle, already out of sight before Mitch had eased his rangy figure back into the light.

"There you are, Mitch!" Amanda exclaimed in delight, her pretty face dimpling.

She was fascinated with Mitch Claydon. Fascinated with everything about him. She prayed he would start paying her more attention. He'd been her escort at the last Outback ball. Of course she'd approached him—put him on the spot, actually—but he could have refused or made up some excuse. He hadn't. He'd even kissed her at the end of that glorious night, putting her in a delirium of excitement and pleasure. Maybe he'd been a tiny bit drunk. All the guys had been. But she was certain he liked her. In some quarters she was very, very popular, but she'd never scored a date with Golden-Boy Claydon. That was what all the girls called him.

Now he was walking towards her, exuding a powerful sexuality. She was certain he'd been with Christine Reardon. Those sparkling blue eyes were alight with arousal and some spark of anger. They'd had an argument, she supposed.

Good!

Nevertheless, Amanda experienced a thrust of jealousy so sharp and so deep it shocked her. Christine Reardon was getting right on her nerves. Wasn't she supposed to have been the great love of his life? Yet she'd left him behind. What woman in her right mind would do that? She'd kill for Mitch Claydon. There was still a deep attachment between them, though. She'd been watching them all night out of the corner of her eye. She couldn't wait for the supermodel to pack her bags and fly off for the Big Apple, or somewhere just as far. The sooner the better. Mitch Claydon was everything any sane woman could ever want.

Quickly, sweetly, Amanda took his arm, her softly voluptuous body blooming. "I'm so enjoying myself, Mitch," she crooned. "I can't thank you enough for inviting me. And Shel, of course. Shel doesn't get out much. She prefers to be at home than out at a party."

"Maybe she's kept far too busy?" Mitch suggested dryly. "It's no secret Shelley works very hard."

"Of course she does," Amanda agreed, sounding mortified. "But she thrives on it. She wouldn't do it otherwise. I must say it's been thrilling to see Christine again. She's so gorgeous, and she doesn't have any airs and graces to her. I love that. We've all missed her. I expect you've missed her too?"

"I certainly have." He hoped that would put Amanda off.

"Wasn't there one time you and she were going to get married?" She glanced up at his marvellous face.

"I don't know how many times you've asked me that, Amanda."

She gave a little breathy laugh. "I guess we're all in awe of Christine. Not everyone gets to be a supermodel. She must have the most glamorous lifestyle—star treatment, all the guys in love with her. Poor old me—I'd be scared of that world myself. Those models try everything! The things you read about them... But Christine knows how to keep her head. She must have had great strength of character, getting off the drugs.''

''What the hell are you talking about?'' Mitch stared down at her.

''Oh, gosh. I've put my foot in it.''

''No need to sound so pleased.''

''Pleased?'' Amanda injected a whole lot of dismay into her voice. ''I'm not pleased. How could you say that, Mitch? But surely you know, or you've heard about it? Why, a few years back Christine admitted in an interview to experimenting with designer drugs. Curiosity, mainly, she said, and obviously she can control it. Some people can, apparently. They take it or leave it. Can't be easy, I tell myself.''

''You're talking absolute rubbish,'' Mitch said flatly.

''Oh, dear. I'm sorry!'' Amanda let out a little woeful cry. ''You're so surprised. I really didn't expect that. I'm fairly certain I've still got the magazine. I thought she was a tiny bit indiscreet, admitting to it, but of course in her world it must be all around her.''

''I dare say it is, but Christine knows how to look after herself. She doesn't do drugs. I'm certain of that. So don't go spreading any damaging gossip. She's denied ever taking them.''

''To you?'' Amanda looked up appealingly. ''Well, she would, wouldn't she? She's not going to risk losing your respect. Anyway, as I say, it was a few years back. She's probably got it out of her system. Please don't be angry, Mitch. I admire Christine as much as you do. But we don't live in her world, so we can't judge her. In the circles she moves in I dare say the temptations are very strong. It's fantastic, too, that she's got this thing going with Ben Savage, the soap star. He's gorgeous!''

"Did you read that too?" Mitch asked in a jaundiced voice.

"Who hasn't?" She giggled. "Apparently they share a very sexual relationship. At any rate, he's following her to Australia. That must be sooo exciting! Squillions of women fantasize about Ben Savage. Me included. Christine must be sizzling with anticipation.''

He slipped his hands into his pockets casually. "I'm surprised she hasn't mentioned it."

"People in the public eye tend to get a little weird about their privacy. They're used to the paparazzi running after them. They adore Christine everywhere. She's a megastar. After the life she's lived she'd find it impossible to settle down back home—not that she will, if Ben Savage has anything to do with it." Amanda laughed gaily, running a playful finger down the sleeve of Mitch's jacket. "If we're very, very lucky we might even get to meet him."

The party went on until around two-thirty a.m., when everyone decided to catch a few hours' sleep.

"Everything okay with you?" Sarah asked Christine very quietly as they walked down the hallway to their rooms. "Under the sparkle I sense upset." Sarah's velvety brown eyes were kind and affectionate and, beyond that, highly perceptive.

"You're an expert at picking it up," Christine said, a wry smile on her mouth. "As a matter of fact Mitch and I had a few words that could easily have got out of hand if we hadn't been interrupted by Amanda. She seems to get into a panic when Mitch is out of her sight."

"She has an enormous crush on him," Sarah confirmed. "What a difference there is between the sisters! Amanda is very pretty, but it's Shelley who touches everyone's heart. She has that little air of valour.''

"Yes," Christine agreed quietly. "She's taken it on her narrow shoulders to look after her family. Such selflessness is rare.''

"I agree. So what about your clash with Mitch? I sensed he was upset as well.''

"He wasn't exactly struggling to get free of Amanda.''

Sarah shook her head. "He doesn't take her seriously, Chris. She's the one making all the effort.''

"Maybe." Christine gave a thin smile. "He did tell me he wasn't going to waste any more of his life on me. That hurt. But it's finally brought home to me just how much I hurt him.''

Sarah put an arm around her friend and hugged her. "You had to leave, Chris. It wasn't what you wanted. It was what you had to do. I can certainly empathize. I kept my deepest secret for years. I caused Kyall great pain.''

"You had your reasons, Sarah. You must have lived a nightmare with none of us to help you. Both you and Kyall suffered because of my grandmother. Were she still alive I think I'd strangle her—'' Christine broke off, a tremor in her voice.

"Kyall told you, of course. About the way Ruth allowed me to believe my baby had died.''

Tears stung Christine's eyes. "What a terrible sin! The whole story shocked me out of my mind. Kyall exposed our grandmother for what she was. A megalomaniac who didn't care for anything outside her own will. Because of her you and Kyall were deprived of the great joy of watching your daughter grow up. I was deprived of a niece. Mum and Dad of a grandchild. It's a miracle that years later you've found her. But one question bothers me, Sarah.

Surely Fiona's adoptive mother must have realized at some point Fiona wasn't her child?''

Sarah assumed a calmness she didn't feel. It was a question she had struggled with on her own. ''If she did, she deliberately blinded herself to it. She loves Fiona. I can forgive her, because our daughter had a happy childhood, and when she's ready she'll come to us—her real parents. It would be too cruel to sever the ties with her adoptive family. Kyall and I don't want that. Fiona loves them as they love her. They'll always be allowed in her life.''

''Which is perhaps more than they deserve, if you look at it from a certain angle,'' Christine said. ''They had their happiness at the expense of yours. It's an extraordinary story, Sarah. Both of us in our way were driven away by my grandmother. There's a happy ending for you and Kyall and your beautiful daughter, but Mitch still doesn't fully understand how it was for me. I laboured all my life for love and approval from my mother and grandmother. Instead I got never-ending criticism.''

''It hasn't embittered you, Chris,'' Sarah assured her, anxious to offer comfort. ''Though understandably it has left its mark. Some childhood scars remain for life. But you've still got the same lovely warm nature. There are considerable similarities between your story and mine. We were both forced to leave the men we loved behind. Both of them found it very difficult battling rejection. Both felt abandoned. Both are proud men.''

''I think in a way Mitch hates me.'' There was a hollow feeling inside Christine's chest. ''He certainly resents me.''

Sarah touched her friend's shoulder. ''That's not true, Chris. I'm sure in his heart he continues to love you, but he's fighting it. He doesn't know your plans. He doesn't know whether he can risk handing over his heart again. He's on guard. A man is just as vulnerable as a woman.

He has just as miserable a time of it when love bonds are broken.'' Sarah sought Christine's eyes. "Can I ask you have you thought ahead to the sort of life you really want? You're famous now. You travel the world. Your photograph is everywhere. Could you turn your back on all that?''

"Tomorrow,'' Christine replied like a shot.

"Are you sure? Your glamorous life over?'' Sarah asked with some gravity.

Christine's smile was almost peaceful. "I've lived it for years now, Sarah. I've found no one to take Mitch's place in my heart. I've had a few serious relationships, thinking they might work. My biological clock is ticking over. I want children, family, a husband—my life partner. I want the sort of things that make a woman feel fulfilled, not to wonder what I missed out on.

"It's not fame. That's very overrated. Or it is in my case. I want to be loved. I want to be the most important person in the world to that special someone. I don't want to finish up lonely. I regard having children as a great achievement, not making the cover of a glossy fashion magazine. By the same token I'm all for a woman having a career *and* marriage, though it seems to be a tall order. I've seen quite a few marriages crash because of career commitments. I guess for it to work both sides have to make compromises. The woman particularly. You're a gifted doctor, but you need Kyall's love. You need your daughter. And I'm sure you and Kyall want more children?''

Sarah nodded. "Oh, yes!''

"Women need to be loved dearly, don't they?''

"Indeed they do.'' Sarah, the doctor and the woman, responded emphatically. "Love bonds are what makes a woman's inner life flourish. Some men can make it on power. Being loved is less significant. But Kyall and Mitch, though they were in a sense handed power at birth, have the same goals as we have. They want a full emotional life. They want wife and family, profound lifetime relationships. Both were devastated when we went away.''

"It wasn't rejection." Christine sought to defend their stand. "We were driven away. Nonetheless, the upshot is that Mitch has developed an inability to ever trust me again.''

"You truly want him?" Sarah gave the younger woman a look of deep seriousness.

"I've never really stopped wanting him," Christine responded with great feeling.

"Then you'll have to convince him of that.''

"If he'll let me. It's not as if I haven't tried.''

"Come on! You've not tried hard enough yet." Sarah said in a bracing tone.

"I suppose it's too much to expect trust can be rebuilt overnight?''

"I prefer to say something positive to you, Chris. Mitch's big and understandable fear is that even if you get back together at some juncture you're going to hanker for the glamorous life you put behind you. His life, his legacy is here on Marjimba, about as far away from the bright lights as one can get. He can't follow you. It's not possible. Not with his history and heritage. You're the one who has to come home. You're the one who'd have to make a series of compromises as women have always done.''

"How would anyone think that would give me a hard time?" Christine's expression contained mild incredulity. "I was born and bred in the bush. I'd never have left had my home life been happy, not decidedly dysfunctional.''

"Forgive me, Chris, but your mother will still be in your life. I know she loves you, but she never learned how to show it.''

''She certainly showed love to Kyall.'' Christine's answer was startlingly intense. ''Adoration was showered on him, by Mum and Gran.''

''He'd have been happier without it, Chris. I know he found all that 'loving' somewhat manic.''

''It was. I was the one who was made to feel of little value. That's why I can identify with Shelley Logan. It's terrible the way she's been made to carry the burden of her twin's death. It must be very painful.''

''It is, but she's no martyr. She has that wonderful thing called spirit. But Pat Logan definitely needs help. He's been in a state of ongoing depression since he buried his little boy. Mrs Logan isn't much better. I see her from time to time. She's so down emotionally when she leaves that even my nerves are screaming.''

''It's a wonder the tourists stay in that atmosphere.''

''They stay because Shelley finds ways to keep them thoroughly entertained. And well fed.''

''If I were Shelley I'd leave.'' Christine opened the door of her room. ''I don't think anyone in her family has the right to push her so far. What's more, if she did, Amanda might have to give herself a great big shake-up. Also, if Amanda's considering Mitch as Prince Charming, she'd better think again. He's mine!''

''Excellent!'' Sarah laughed.

''Believe me—'' Christine planted an affectionate kiss on Sarah's cheek ''—real love does last. It's just taken me a while to realize it.''

CHAPTER SEVEN

CHRISTINE flipped back and forth in her bed during the few hours she had of sleep. Her fragmented dreams were all of heated conversations with Mitch, in which the infatuated Amanda was standing off in the wings, striking attitudes that indicated she was totally on Mitch's side. A psychologist would find it all too simple to analyse: she was frightened she wouldn't be able to regain Mitch's trust, and her fear was compounded by the possibility he might turn to Amanda for female company and support.

Finally, at dawn, she fought out of the dream sequences stuck on replay. She threw back the bedclothes, went to the adjoining bathroom and took a quick shower to wash away the cobwebs. Afterwards she put on a T-shirt, jeans and her riding boots, gathering up her cream akubra as she let herself out of her bedroom door. The carpeted hallway was still softly lit, the packed household dreaming the dawn away.

At the stables she greeted and petted the glossy-flanked Wellington, who acted as pleased to see her as she was to see him. Saddled up, she rode out, the reins easily gathered in her left hand as she stooped to open then shut a side gate. She intended heading in the direction of the chain of billabongs that flowed through the station—always her favourite ride.

It was magic this time of morning. The great silence was broken by the dawn ritual of birdsong that began with little peeps and chirrups, gradually turning into a powerful cacophony of sound, like musical instruments tuning up for

119

the greatest orchestra on earth. There were the high, sweet strings, wonderful cello notes, resonant woodwinds, golden brass, and they all came together in a magnificent symphony that carried for miles across the open plains and into the desert.

As she rode, the indigos, pinks and golds piled up on the horizon slowly vanished and the sky took on the brilliance of blue crystal. In the distance, across the spinifex-shrouded flats that so resembled wheat, she could see a long trailing cloud of red dust that signalled the approach of a mob of Marjimba cattle.

She wondered how long a delay there would be before Mitch found a replacement for Jack Cody, who was known to be furious at his dismissal. Julanne had told her over morning tea. Cody had been sacked without a reference, but paid right up. By now he'd be back on the road, looking for another stockman's job, although his final comment to Mitch had been, "I'll be back!"

If it had been meant as a threat Mitch didn't act as if he was worried.

She blushed to think she had seriously considered going down to Mitch's room last night. The only thing that had saved her was not maidenly concern about her provocative behaviour but the fact the homestead was full of guests. Besides, she didn't actually know what Amanda was capable of. Word was, Amanda was a man-stealer—or such was her reputation. Apparently she had stolen her best friend's boyfriend. That had to be some sort of an indication.

Putting such thoughts out of her head, Christine rode through the radiant morning, letting the big gelding have its head in an exhilarating gallop before heading towards the nearby lagoon. There was music too in the running water, in the frilly white ripples as they ran swiftly around boulders and cascaded over rocks. She hitched the chestnut gelding to a branch, watching him bend his glistening neck to the green undergrowth, tearing at it with big strong teeth, chewing contentedly.

With a feeling of relaxation Christine moved off, following the woody trail that cut a swathe down the slope to the sand. Wattles and paper barks draped their branches overhead, some of the trees festooned with the climbing wild passionflower.

A flight of ducks—teal and wood ducks and the scarlet-hooded, orange-breasted lotus birds, the "lily trotters"—had alighted on the emerald surface of the lagoon, floating in and out of the pink water lilies and the spears of aquatic grasses that thickly fringed the perimeter. The vivid green reeds were intermingled with tall, delicate white day lilies in flower that gave off an exquisitely sweet perfume. She breathed it in, thinking such a fragrance had never yet been matched in a bottle.

It was such a peaceful scene it released all her pressures. Sometimes the beauty of nature was almost too much for her. She remembered as a child feeling joy to the point of welling tears at all the splendour, the sound and colour around her, the sweet and aromatic scents of the bush. She understood the wilderness. It was as though she'd never been away.

The lilied stretch of shining water danced before her. The sun glinted off myriad birds' feathers, throwing out flashes of iridescent greens, silvers and reds from neck and wing. There was an enormous concentration of water birds in her heartland, the Channel Country, a natural feature that made the vast area so compelling. The ducks were floating so smoothly the overhanging trees made clear-cut reflections in the water.

Christine sat down quietly on a weathered grey boulder,

staring in silent wonder at the scene before her. Moments like this were akin to having God place a calming hand on her shoulder. Bring order to your life, Christine, for life is a miracle. She knew it. These lagoons were precious sanctuaries in the vast arid isolation, and wonderful places to gain insight.

Surely she'd had long enough to know what it took to make her happy? She'd enjoyed what often seemed to her a fantasy career, involving as it did living the so-called "good life". But in recent times she had come to the full realization that she didn't want to be a player. She wanted commitment. A much greater wholeness.

As a girl she had been so deeply in love with Mitch and he with her it had seemed as if they were one. They had often spoken of their sense of oneness as being like two separate streams flowing into the one river. But at some stage of her under-development—as she thought of it—she had realized their relationship mightn't work out unless she quelled all the undercurrents that threatened and overwhelmed her young life.

Her grandmother Ruth, more than anyone, had thrown such a shadow over her. Even her mother had forever been trying to change her. There was a great deal of angst still inside her. It stirred the moment she and her mother were reunited. For all her success she was still vulnerable to her mother's insensitive comments. She supposed she always would be. It was a fact of life that had to be accepted.

Kyall wanted her at home. The homestead was a mansion by anyone's standards—even her super-rich friends'—and there was plenty of room for all of them without invading anyone else's privacy. But Kyall would soon be married. Sarah would be mistress of Wunnamurra, with all that entailed. Christine couldn't think her mother would take all that easily to the big shift in her position. The fact of the matter was that Enid, though she would have denied it with her last breath, was relishing being Numero Uno now that her own mother, Ruth, was gone.

Then there was her promise to Suzanne. Christine fully intended to live up to that. Suzanne had been dealt a rough hand, losing her parents at such an early age. It was her great hope—and she knew Kyall and Sarah felt the same— that Suzanne and Fiona would form a strong, loving relationship. McQueen blood ran in their veins.

Kyall had offered to let Christine in on the business: McQueen Enterprises. She knew, especially in view of her own portfolio, that she had a good business brain—inherited, no doubt, but she also knew there was no real future without Mitch. He held her happiness in the palm of his hand. She had forced herself to leave him once. She couldn't leave him again. Success had proved fragile. Loving Mitch had assumed central importance in her life. She couldn't accept she had ruined their once wonderful relationship.

She had a few loose ends to tie up before she could come home to roost. A fashion commitment in Sydney—a series of parades for a leading department store—a quick trip overseas, to say her goodbyes, then she could embark on the next, potentially the most exciting stage of her life.

"Onward, Christine!" In her enthusiasm she spoke aloud, shocked out of her reverie as a figure detached itself from the scrub. She was on her feet instantly, every muscle alert.

"Why, if it isn't the posh Miss Reardon, talking to herself," Jack Cody, the ex-overseer called in a slurred, sneering voice. "I hate rich, pampered women," he muttered, half staggering down the slope.

Christine flashed her eyes, indignant. Was he drunk at this hour of the morning? "What are you doing around here, Cody?'' she challenged, wondering if he were dangerous. She would know soon enough. ''You were sacked a week ago.''

''Hell, I'm just takin' my time,'' he growled. ''What did I do, anyway, that big-shot Claydon had to show me the door? I coulda taken care of that bloody brumby.''

''Are you nuts? The brumby would have taken care of you—or any one of us.''

''Typical female response!'' Cody chortled. ''Made no damn sense Claydon killed 'im.''

''It was necessary.''

''Guess you're Claydon's number one fan.''

''Which is none of your business. If you want real trouble you won't attempt to intimidate me. I advise you to get on your way.''

''Problem is, you've seen me.''

''I wouldn't have seen you if you hadn't broken cover. And you're drunk.''

''Wrong. I was drunk last night. It was pretty bloody cold, but I'm dead sober this mornin'. Anyone tell you you got the bluest eyes? Now look at you. Long hair in a braid, breasts shovin' against that little T-shirt. I reckon you're the best-lookin' woman I've ever laid eyes on.''

''Go away, Cody.'' Fury and an element of primitive fear stuck in Christine's throat. Cody was a big man, lean and fit, but there was real evidence he was still under the effects of alcohol. If he approached her she would make a break for it.

His heavy steps grew nearer. ''Don't be scared. I'm not gonna hurt you. Steal a kiss, maybe. I've always been bold with the ladies. Nothin' ventured, et cetera et cetera...''

''Back off!'' Her anger grew. ''I'm Mitch Claydon's friend, remember? We're talking about a guy you should watch out for.''

His grimace held an unnerving amount of resentment. "So what's Claydon gonna do? Beat me to a pulp? It'd be worth it just to have a conversation with you." He looked her up and down in a way that made her hands clench.

"Sorry!" Her voice was cold and hard. "I'm not talking. Do what I say—back off."

He smiled, as though he was humouring her. "Keep it together, lady. Keep cool. It looks like you're in for that kiss. After that, no problem."

Everything about him made her doubt that—the focus of his eyes, the stupid bombastic smile.

She moved suddenly, kicking up sand and watching it spray against his chest and face, stinging his eyes.

"Hey, you shouldn't have done that." He rubbed at his eyes, doing more damage, then reached out a long arm for her.

Christine pulled away violently, kicking up more sand, grimly satisfied to see it find its mark. She had a few seconds to get past him, then tear up the slope. She had never been physically frightened by a man in her life, but she was now, her heart pounding in her ribs as she ran.

Of course he followed her, bellowing that he wasn't going to touch her. "Are you crazy? Stop—we can sort this out."

She didn't think so. She had seen the excitement in his eyes. A woman was vulnerable all the time, and Cody was too turned on by her for his own good. Therefore he was very dangerous.

Drunk or not, he was fast and agile. She increased her pace, stumbled twice. A low branch whipped her face but she felt no pain. Halfway up the slope he made a huge grab for her, but she turned, lashing him across the face with the open palm of her hand.

"Are you sure you want to make a fight of it?" He was

loving it, exuding cocky power, his eyes peeling the clothes off her.

"You're the one who'll find yourself in trouble." She was panting, sweat breaking out on her and flushing her cheeks. "I'm meeting up with Mitch. He'll come looking."

"You don't expect me to believe you, do yah?" This time he clamped a strong hand to her shoulder.

His expression, unmistakably carnal, and the tone of his voice outraged her, momentarily overcoming her panic. "Stop now, Cody," she warned, anger and revulsion ripping through her. "I'll report this. You'll never find work again."

"Hey, that's a lot to lose." He jerked her closer, staring at her mouth. "Listen, I told yah I have the solution. One kiss. Somethin' tells me you're a terrific kisser. One kiss and I swear I'll back off. That's if you want me to. A lotta women find me attractive."

The strange confidence in his voice nauseated her. Her whole body tensed, as though she were about to ward off a physical blow.

"Not me."

She forced her breath to calm. She could scream her head off but no one would hear her. And as soon as she started screaming he would try to overpower her, clamping a hand across her mouth. Not that he would need to bother. The water birds, disturbed, would take to the air in great confusion, creating their own tumult of sound.

His fingers were inside her T-shirt, pulling at her bra strap. "You're stunning, you know that? I don't mind a bit you're so tall." Smilingly he bent towards her, so she could smell the stale whisky on his breath. "Don't worry, I'm not gonna hurt yah. I think you're gonna like it. We'll both like it."

Christine had resolved her actions. She brought up her knee so hard it was an explosion in his groin.

He fell back with a yell so filled with pain he might have been tortured, but Christine didn't stop to watch him go into a huddle as he tried to cope with that pain. With an abrupt burst of speed she took off, oblivious to his moans and obscenities.

"Bitch! You're not gonna be safe now."

"Don't move." A man was standing about ten feet away from Christine, emanating such menace there might have been danger flags flapping all around him. To Christine he said, very quietly but succinctly, "Get out of here."

Her relief was such it was excruciating. "I'm not going anywhere, Mitch. I'm too concerned about you."

"Ain't nuthin'," Cody called in a hoarse, urgent voice. "Just a bit of fun." There was no question from his demeanour that he had been thoroughly intimidated from the moment Mitch stepped out of the thicket of trees.

"The fun hasn't started." Mitch kept his eyes on Cody while he walked towards Christine.

"I can explain!" Cody yelled, scrambling to stand straight.

"Nothing happened, Mitch." Christine gazed, perturbed, into Mitch's taut face, alarmed by something in his manner. He had the look of a man about to pound Cody to pulp.

"Get on your horse, Chris, and ride away," he ordered, without looking at her. "This is between Cody and me."

"Dammit, the lady's right!" Cody wheezed, still trying to cope with the pain in his groin. "I did nuthin'."

"That's right, you didn't—because you didn't have time," Mitch said, sounding almost friendly. "Now we've got all the time in the world."

Cody stared up at him, amazed to realise he was capable

of being frightened. "Hold on, man! Wait one damn minute," he appealed.

Mitch glanced at Christine with sizzling blue eyes. "I won't say it again, Christine. Go home. This has nothing to do with you now."

She shook her head hard. "Never! I'm not going to ride away while you're in any sort of danger."

For a moment he almost laughed. "You've been away too long, Chrissy. There's no need for your concern, but it's nice to know it's there. I know how to look after myself. I also know how to take care of a guy like Cody—who, incidentally has been stealing our stock with a few of his mates. The maximum penalty for stock theft is now ten years, Cody," he called. "Why would you be fool enough to try it on Marjimba? Obviously you haven't been with us long enough to know I organise plenty of checks. Especially when a character like you supposedly pulls out."

"Try to prove it." Cody showed a flicker of bravado.

"Already have. I've had a stock squad officer working the station for days now. He found your portable yard, your mates and our stock. It was easy to connect up the road train. Cattle theft is costing us station owners three million a year in this state alone. What a fool you were to get yourself involved."

Cody shook his head, held up a hand. "Weren't substantial."

"Substantial enough. You know what you've done, Cody. You've mucked up your life. Especially since you decided to bother Miss Reardon. We have to come together on that."

Cody cleared his throat, his lean cheeks so sunken he looked like a stunned wolf. "Stay away from me, Claydon. Your girlfriend's already nearly killed me with a knee in the groin. Hell, I wasn't gonna hurt her. I just wasn't. I don't do rape. Just wanted to kiss her. Dammit, lady, tell him.'' Cody appealed to Christine, who put her hand on Mitch's arm, feeling the tight bunch of muscle.

"Let him go, Mitch. He's not worth it.''

"Can't say I can.'' Mitch began to walk purposefully down the slope.

"Go on—hit me. Go ahead and do it,'' Cody invited, watching Mitch's formidable approach, almost admiring it. "I don't give a damn.''

"No kidding?'' Without wasting another minute Mitch rammed his fist into Cody's jaw, stepping back fastidiously as Cody dropped like a stone not about to rise.

"Oh, God!'' Christine moved frantically, reaching Mitch's side within seconds. "You're not going to hit him again?''

"Why bother? I think he's out for the count.'' His frosty eyes coolly swept her. "Do you ever do anything you're told?''

"Hey, don't turn on me. I didn't want to see you get hurt.''

He shot her a mocking look. "No chance of that—but since you're here you can do something. You can get me a rope. There's one in the Jeep. It's back through the trees. You can't miss it. I have to tie Cody up.''

She stooped over the prone man. "There's blood drooling down his chin.''

"Tough beans! Are you going to get the rope?''

"You bet I am.'' She started to move. "What are you going to do with him?''

"Catapult him into the creek? Hang him? I'm open to suggestions. No, I think the stock police can take him away.''

"I don't think he would have hurt me,'' she assured Mitch nervously.

"Oh, hell, no!" He didn't sound convinced.

"Besides, I'd almost managed to get away."

"You're a smart woman."

"I am. I'm fairly sure he wouldn't have made a serious move on me."

"Yeah, well, that's not good enough," said Mitch. "Because if he'd hurt you I'd have had to kill him."

By mid-afternoon most of the guests had gone home after a sumptuous al fresco brunch. The only ones remaining were Kyall and Sarah and the Logan sisters. The Saunderses who had arrived with Kyall, had cadged a ride on an earlier flight out.

Cody's arrest had caused a minor sensation. They had all watched him, pinned between two burly stock police and bundled into a four-wheel drive. Between them Christine and Mitch had agreed not to mention Christine's brush with him at the lagoon—his man-handling of her or Cody's panic-stricken reaction when Mitch had arrived.

In the big airy bedroom—the very best guest room at Marjimba Homestead—Christine double-checked the wardrobe and drawers to see she hadn't left anything behind. She was going home with Kyall. There was no point at all in Mitch making a separate trip.

Though the Cody incident had upset her, it could have been much, much worse had Mitch not arrived. She was determined on putting it to the back of her mind. She had thoroughly enjoyed her stay on Marjimba. It had been a beautiful, liberating time. But now she had to go home to her mother, and their problematic relationship. She had so wanted to mend it, but she'd have to work harder to make it happen. Her mother was one difficult woman but Christine was determined to be cheerful in her outlook.

There was one other dark cloud on the home front.

Christine was unable to forget Kyall's shocked revelation that their father might have formed a serious relationship with a woman in the town. Though he had certainly suffered a lack of tenderness and attention from his own wife.

When a tap came at her door she went to it all smiles, expecting to see Julanne. Instead Mitch stood on the threshold. "May I come in?" he asked, his eyes licking at her sensitive flesh.

She couldn't face him without wanting to fall into his arms. "You'd never have to force my bedroom door open, Mitch," she answered, standing back while he walked past her, his bright aura lighting up the whole room.

"Is that so?" He turned back to study her. "That's odd. When I made it to your door last night it was locked."

"You're joking?" Should she tell him of her own trembling desire to go to *his* bed?

"Honestly—I made it to your door, then I thought better of it." His eyes danced wickedly.

"So you walked by? Maybe down to Amanda's?" The surge of hope died quickly.

"Chrissy, darling, I think you've stretched this thing with Amanda to twanging point." He came back to her and brushed his fingertips across her cheek. "That poor girl needs a job to occupy her mind. All she does is sit around looking pretty." Now his fingers were in her long hair.

"It's a wonder she doesn't feel guilty, with her sister working so hard."

"She doesn't feel guilty, believe me." Mitch's voice was dry. He dropped his hand, though he was in a hot haze of desire all over again. "So, have you enjoyed your stay?"

"I've had the loveliest time!" Christine's beautiful smile flashed. "Your mother is more of a mother to me than my own."

"That's sad, though I rejoice in the fact Mum has always

treated you like family. Drawing on recent observations, I can't see the troubled relationship between you and your mother changing.'' He sank into a chair, thinking how immaculately groomed she always was.

"Lord knows I want it to.''

"Sometimes wanting can't make it so. That's the way life is.''

"I think she loves me in her own way.'' Christine's expression was soft and vulnerable, sweeping him back years, to when she had been so desperate for approval.

"One would hope so.'' He spoke quietly but bitterly. It amazed and angered him, the scars left on Christine. "So, how long are you going to stay around?''

She sat down on the side of the bed, facing him. "I have a commitment to do a series of fashion parades in Sydney in a couple of weeks' time. And I want to catch up with Suzanne while I'm there. She needs some tender loving care. Then I have to tie up a few loose ends.''

"Like Ben Savage?'' He cursed himself when it came out so hard-edged.

"What's Ben got to do with it?'' she asked in surprise.

"You tell me.'' His eyes had darkened to turquoise, a sure sign he was disturbed.

"You sound like you're expecting some announcement?'' Challenge was passing from one to the other, hot and swift.

"Isn't he coming to Australia? I heard he was going to be in Sydney while you're there?''

"Most probably he will be,'' she agreed, breathing deeply to keep her equilibrium.

"So you knew about it?''

"What is this? The third degree? I know Ben's doing a trip to publicize his show. He's very popular in Australia. Your own mother watches the show.''

"I wouldn't say she's an addict." He pushed his hands behind his head. "At least I hope she isn't. It's pretty damned silly."

"So you watch it?" she asked sweetly. "That's fabulous!"

"Sorry, sweetheart, I'm not that pleasure-deprived. Ben, according to the tabloids, is always trying to find true love. I thought it was with you?"

She suppressed the urge to snap. "Ben is a nice guy. You'd like him."

"Not if you were his wife," he clipped. "Or even his girlfriend."

"I'm an ex-girlfriend."

"Does he know the difference?" Mitch watched her eyes. "Didn't he say somewhere his love for you just wouldn't die?"

Christine grimaced. "I think that's one of the recurring lines in his scripts."

Restlessly Mitch stood up, walking to the open French doors and staring out at the sunlit garden. "Does he do drugs?"

Christine's lustrous dark head shot up. "Why ever do you ask that? Not everyone in the business does. Ben's too damned smart."

"But you know a lot of people who do?"

"Of course. Let's face it."

"And you've never been tempted?"

"Listen, I've damned well told you I haven't. I wouldn't have thought I'd have to tell you again. Surely you know that much about me?" Precipitately Christine stood up, wondering if someone might have been trying to trash her reputation. "What is this all about, Mitch?"

"Is that a no?" Mitch asked.

"Go to hell!" She felt her temper snap. "I thought we'd

had this discussion. Obviously someone's been talking to you, haven't they? Some mutual friend who wanted to share a scandalous secret?''

"Celebrities do get talked about.''

"Was it dear Amanda by any chance?'' she queried, her eyes stormy. "I wouldn't put it past her. So what did she say? She read some place that Christine Reardon admits to having fun with designer drugs?''

"Something like that.'' He shrugged.

"And you believed it?'' She was so hurt and angry she felt like taking a swing at him.

"Actually, I didn't. I know quite a lot about you, Chrissy. You've always had character.''

"So why are you trying to get me riled up?'' she asked in amazement.

"Just checking.''

Her expression went from surprise to disgust. "Oh, thank you.''

"I didn't intend to insult you. Forgive me if I have. I hadn't realized Amanda was quite so dangerous.''

"Perhaps you should take a closer look at her when she's not wearing her flirty red dress. Obviously she believes all's fair in love and war. That was a vicious lie. I think I'll have a few words with her.''

"I think you should. That's why I told you. So, this is goodbye for a while?'' He came towards her, his gaze so intense she swallowed.

"God, Mitch, I hope not. My holiday isn't over.''

"You'll be flying away from me for the rest of your life.''

"Is it so hard for you to accept I'm at a turning point in my life, Mitch?'' She looked up with appeal in her eyes.

"So am I!'' he answered with quiet force. "It usually happens around thirty.''

"Hey, I'm twenty-eight." She tried to lighten him up.

"And I've never seen anyone look more fabulous. But let's get this straight. Are you asking me to consider the possibility you're coming home for good rather than living your dream?" He sent the expression up, and did it very well.

"Why so sarcastic?"

He stared into her beautiful eyes. "There's a good deal of pain around the whole issue, Chrissy. What do you say I come visit when you're in Sydney? A little house-call?"

She was overwhelmed, his blue gaze bathing her in simmering heat. "Are you serious? Could you get away?"

"I think so." He could have said that if he thought there was a chance of resuming their old relationship he'd travel to the ends of the earth, but he didn't. He was endlessly on guard. "I still care, Chrissy, but the trouble is I can't trust your good intentions."

That brought her back to earth with a jolt. "You might if you stopped talking about the past. I'm looking to the future."

"With me in it?" A cynical smile played about his mouth.

"Of course." She sighed heavily. "I care about you too, Mitch. That's why I'm not at all happy with your talking about me behind my back."

He laughed. "So you think I should have slugged Amanda like I slugged Cody? I don't hit women."

"I forgot. You kiss them." All of a sudden she thought briefly, furiously, of the number of women he had probably kissed. And he was a great kisser.

"I'm about to kiss you." He reached out and caught her wrist, the little callused pads on his fingers sending quivers along her skin.

"Make it deep and passionate so I can remember it."

"I will. Don't worry." In one breathtaking sweep he gathered her in with one arm, lowering his mouth over hers. "I want it all," he murmured. "I want everything about you."

She could have fainted away, her level of excitement was so great. She could feel the sweet heaviness in her breasts, at the pit of her stomach. She reached up her arms to clasp them behind his neck, wanting more of his mouth, more of his tongue, of the warm, lean, hard body that held her so tightly.

She was all yearning, desire swirling in her blood like a flash flood. She could feel his hands running down over her body as though he wanted to tear her clothes from her. She didn't care. She was encouraging him with funny little whimpers she didn't recognise as her own.

"Oh, Mitch, darling!" That cry of hers was full of longing.

His mouth was dragging down over her face, across her hot cheeks to her pulsing lips. He was breathing something into her mouth she couldn't quite hear because there was such a tumult in her. Endearments?

"I want everything."

Their kisses and caresses intensified, her fingers and nails kneading his taut flesh. Where was this going? Another minute and they'd be on the bed. Wasn't that what she wanted more than anything in the world?

Want and nothing more! The longing alone was excruciating.

She was all tousled hair, scarlet-cheeked, panting, her shirt swinging open from the slow sliding of his hands over her breasts, when a knock on the door shocked them back to reality.

"Oh, God, I don't believe this!"

"Steady, steady..." he cautioned.

Frantically she set about buttoning up her shirt. There was no time to tuck it in. She had to let it hang loose.

Mitch ran a ruthless hand through his golden locks. "Looks like the only way I can have you is to take you out bush."

"Don't think I won't come," she promised, a wry little smile about her mouth. "Hang on!" she called, as the knock came a second time. "Do I look all right?" she appealed to Mitch, her face flushed and filled with heart-wrenching excitement.

"Thoroughly kissed, but that's fine." That was the way to handle Chris. Kiss her senseless. "It's probably Mum."

It was. Julanne, smiling a little uncertainly, stood outside the door. She took one look at Christine's radiant rosy face, then glanced beyond her to her son. "What's life without romance?" She smiled with emphasis and warmth.

"Speaking for myself, no fun at all," Mitch moved with indolent grace to where his mother was standing. He patted her gently on the cheek. "I was just telling Chris how much we've enjoyed her stay."

"Indeed we have." Julanne looked from one to the other. "There will be other times, surely, before you have to go back to Sydney, Chris?"

"There was talk of a fundraiser for the hospital," she said, turning to snap her last piece of luggage shut and regain her composure at the same time. "Sarah came up with the idea of a polo match-picnic. It will be held on Wunnamurra." Another excuse to see Mitch.

"Kyall hasn't said a word about it."

"It's not finalised yet." She turned back to him brightly. "But he will. You're his best player."

"No better than Kyall. Then we'll get to see you again pretty soon?"

She was aware she blushed. "I'll make sure of it."

* * *

There was no time for Christine to have a private word with Amanda until they landed on Wybourne Station, fifty miles as the crow flies to the south-east of Marjimba.

No one was around to meet them. The whole place had a look of quiet desolation, though Christine knew from experience there were numerous beauty spots across the large sheep and cattle station. An open Jeep was parked in the shade of the empty hangar and Kyall, flanked by Sarah and Shelley, walked towards it to see if the keys were in the ignition. It was years now, Christine had learned, since Patrick Logan had been forced to sell his Cessna.

"I really did think Dad would be down here to meet us," Amanda said crossly, shading her eyes. "He hardly does anything for us any more."

"He hasn't had any treatment for his condition all this time?" Christine asked in a kindly, concerned voice.

"What condition?" Amanda jerked back as though bitten by a death adder.

"I'm sorry, but there can't be a more terrible thing than to lose one's child," Christine apologized. "Little Sean was so loved, depression must have settled over your parents."

"And there's a cure for depression?" Amanda asked in a bitter, resentful tone. "It's been years now, not yesterday. Other people rebuild their lives. Mum and Dad simply turned off the engines."

Christine studied the young woman in front of her with a measure of dismay. "How terribly sad, Amanda. But there are anti-depressant medicines, counselling, methods for survival. You must help your parents do something about it. At some stage in our lives all of us are going to need help."

"Dad won't take any help from anyone," Amanda said in a surprisingly hard tone. "Mum sees Sarah from time to time. I grieved myself, though I was only small, but no one worries about me."

"I'm sure they do," Christine assured her. "But, as you said yourself, you were young, Amanda. A child in development. You had time to work it through. I'm talking about your parents. And Shelley. Everyone says she works so hard."

Amanda frowned, as though she wasn't at all sure about that. "Everyone is very concerned about my sister and how she copes with all the pressures. I say it gives her a chance to make up for what she did."

Christine felt herself recoil in shock. She stared into Amanda's pretty face, chilled and disbelieving. These were sisters. She would have loved a sister. "What she did?" she echoed. "It could have been you, Amanda, who walked away and left the twins unattended."

Amanda turned on her fiercely, powerfully outraged. "That's not true!"

"You're too ready to blame your sister." Christine had heard the crack of jealousy in Amanda's tone. "She's had to shoulder the burden of guilt for most of her life."

"Have you considered she deserves it?" Amanda stood her ground, terrible memories stirred up.

Christine felt herself swallow hard. "I can't believe you said that."

"She pushed him in. Saved herself." Amanda's eyes flashed, seemingly without compassion.

"Or you were there, perhaps, too late?"

For a moment Amanda's expression went absolutely blank. "I can't believe you're blaming me," she said finally. "Shel was always getting into trouble for being naughty. She was hyperactive, just like she is today."

"I've heard she's making quite a success of the tourist scheme," Christine pointed out loyally.

''Do you really think she doesn't have help? I do all I can. I may not roll my sleeves up and get dirty, but I have talents Shel doesn't possess. Anyway, I really don't want to talk about this, Christine. I don't even know where you're coming from. You're a stranger these days. It's our tragedy, not yours.''

''Then you shouldn't spend so much time keeping it alive,'' Christine responded without hesitation. ''By the way I'm not standing here in the hot sun talking to you for nothing.''

''No, you're being deliberately offensive.'' Anger beat in waves around Amanda.

''I am, in fact, being quite restrained. I have a bone to pick with you, Amanda.''

''I'm sure I can deal with it,'' Amanda snapped.

''You'd be a fool if you didn't. You told Mitch you'd read an article about me in which I admitted to having been a drug-user?''

Amanda's full lips parted, but for a few telling seconds no sound came out. ''Mitch told you?'' she croaked discordantly.

''Indeed he did. Mitch and I are very close. We have been since childhood.''

''That's interesting!'' Amanda's expression sharpened. ''Because Mitch told me he hadn't thought of you in years. You chose your course. You were out of his life. Did he tell you that?''

''Amanda, I don't believe Mitch said that at all. You're just trying to make trouble. It could be one of your flaws.''

Amanda stared back as though mesmerized. ''Hey, why are you attacking me in this way?''

''Think of it as my defending my reputation.'' Christine continued to stare into Amanda's eyes, refusing to allow her gaze to slide away. ''You can't lie about me and get away with it. I'll take action. I might have a word with your parents if I have to.''

''You wouldn't.'' Amanda lost some of her high colour.

''Try me. I'm going to ask Sarah to keep her ears open for any ugly little rumours circulating regarding me or my lifestyle. I hope I make myself clear?''

It was obvious Amanda hadn't been prepared for this particular confrontation. ''I can't see why you're adopting this attitude,'' she said, suddenly drawing on tears from her arsenal. ''I thought I read it. I apologize unreservedly if I got it wrong.''

Always the liar. ''Just stick to the truth, Amanda. That's good advice. Now, if you'll excuse me, I'd like to have a word with Shelley.''

''Our little work freak!'' Amanda laughed scornfully. ''I hope you're as unpleasant to her as you've been to me.''

Christine regarded the other woman without expression. ''With a sister like you she doesn't need anyone else to offer unkindness.'' Turning her back, Christine walked away.

CHAPTER EIGHT

A COUPLE of days home and Christine missed Mitch as a woman stranded in the desert would miss water. Kyall had Sarah, the two of them exuding happiness through their very pores. They had heard yesterday—and it was a matter for great celebration—that Fiona would finally be coming home to Wunnamurra two weeks before the wedding. Christine didn't want to dwell on how the Hazeltons, the couple who had reared Fiona as their own, would be feeling. They would be devastated—in a manner of speaking tasting the grief of bereavement.

So many bad things seemed to have started and ended with her grandmother. Ruth had damaged not only her family but many people around her, including the Hazeltons. The good thing was Kyall and Sarah had found it in their hearts to allow Fiona and her adoptive parents time to make this huge adjustment, making the promise that Fiona would always be free to visit the couple who had reared her.

Christine was looking forward immensely to meeting her niece, and had high hopes that Fiona and Suzanne, who had never really had a home, would "click". If Fiona were anything like Sarah, her mother, with Sarah's kindness and sensitivity, she would be a great support for the troubled Suzanne.

On the third morning Christine enjoyed her usual early-morning ride, coming home to surprise her parents having a rip-roaring argument. Their voices floated out of the study, carrying along the passageway into the entrance hall. Christine was astounded. She had rarely heard her parents argue. In fact she could count the number of times on one hand. Her father was a highly civilised man, perhaps too civilised for his own good. He had always allowed her mother to have her way. His only interventions over the years had been to stand by his daughter against her grandmother Ruth and Enid.

She had no wish to embarrass them, so she started to tiptoe across the marbled expanse to the staircase, almost reaching it before her mother, tears pouring down her face, obviously unable to control herself, dashed into sight.

Christine was horrified. "Mum, what's the matter?" Her mother rarely cried.

"Out of my way, Christine." Enid was shaking with anger, almost berserk.

"Can't I help?" This struck her as pathetic. Her formidable mother in fits of weeping?

Enid, a bundle of nerves, rounded on her, looking as if she wanted to kick and scream. "Your father wants to leave me," she cried at the top of her lungs.

"Oh, my God!" Why hadn't she guessed it was coming? Kyall had warned her.

"Is that all you can say?" Enid cried wildly. "'Oh, my God'? We can't put pressure on Him." Her handsome face was working, as were her twisting hands. "You always were on your father's side."

"Oh, Mum, that's not fair. I'm so, so sorry." Why couldn't there be understanding between them?

"You're sorry?" Enid's brilliant dark eyes flashed, making her look momentarily like her own mother, Ruth. "How do you think I feel? I've done everything—looked after him—for thirty-three years. And he's betrayed me with some wicked bitch in town. The shame of it! Thank God your grandmother is not here to see it."

The hypocrisy was too much for Christine. "Leave Gran

out of it,'' she said crisply. "I've heard all about her ex-
ploits. Words don't express the damage Gran did. She
treated Dad badly. She used to talk about 'looking after'
him, too. It was a myth. Dad has worked long and hard for
Wunnamurra. And you.''

"So! We know where *you* stand,'' Enid exclaimed bitterly. "Always sticking up for your father. I see it as treachery on your part.'' Enid suddenly collapsed onto a step,
letting her head fall into her hands.

"I'm very concerned about you too, Mum.'' Cautiously
Christine approached her. "I don't want to see you hurt
and humiliated.''

Enid shot up her head, gesturing for Christine to be quiet.
"To think your father has been having a sexual relationship
with another woman! I can't get over it.'' She gave a thin,
slightly hysterical laugh.

"Why not, Mum?'' Christine sat down quietly on the
step beside her mother. "It's really astonishing the way you
believe that because you can function well enough without
a sex-life so can Dad. He's a fit, healthy, handsome man.''

"He's *my husband*,'' Enid shouted, as though everything
else was of no consequence.

"That doesn't make him your slave.''

"Don't talk to me like that, young lady,'' Enid said in
a voice so sharp it would have made anyone jump. "I don't
like it. I demand respect. I imagine you've seen pretty well
everything these last years, away from your good home,
but we do things differently here. Marriage vows are sacred. There has never been a divorce in our family.''

"Are you worried about the scandal, or losing Dad?''
Christine countered, amazed she and her mother hadn't
come to blows.

"I won't lose him.'' Enid set her jaw. "I refuse to let
him go.''

"I'm so sorry, Mum, but you can't force Dad to stay."

"You're dead wrong about that."

"How?"

"By making it impossible for him to live. Certainly not on McQueen territory, or in the style he's become accustomed to."

"I doubt he wants any of it," Christine said, thinking her father would have all the financial support he wanted from her. "Who is this woman he wants to leave you for?"

A raised vein in Enid's temple throbbed. "He won't tell me, but I'll find out. She has to be crazy if she thinks she can walk over me. I'll kill her."

"That's not only stupid, Mum, it's ugly. You've all but handed Dad over to her on a platter. You've sidelined him without a thought. Surely having separate bedrooms is a rebuff?"

Enid responded fiercely. "That's absolutely none of your business."

"Maybe not, but it seems to me you might start thinking about how you lost him. Or how much you're going to fight to get him back. It'll be a fair fight, I hope."

Enid put her hands over her ears while Christine was talking, removing them when she stopped. "What would you know about marital problems?" she jeered. "Aren't you the one who lost Mitchell Claydon? I've been a great wife and a great mother. I am shockingly, horribly disappointed in you and your father, Christine. It seems after all I've done for you both neither of you cares about me. Why don't you go to your father now?" she urged angrily. "He's in the study. And with our thirty-fourth anniversary coming up. The timing! Talk about treachery! He says she's a lovely person. Can you beat that? Did you know your father was sleeping around?"

Christine stood up, wondering if her relationship with her

mother was going to be as bad in adult life as it had been in her childhood and adolescence. "Why don't you talk to Kyall about it?" she suggested quietly. "He's your favourite, remember? I'm only Christine. I will go and talk to Dad. Despite my best intentions my conversations with you always turn into a disaster. Still, I'm sorry, Mum. Your happiness is important to me."

"Oh, go away!" Enid cried vehemently. "You've never loved me, Christine. We're totally different kinds of people. But my son won't tolerate my suffering."

Christine found her father sitting behind his desk, as quiet as her mother was frantic.

"Gosh, Dad, what have you done?" She shut the door behind her and took a seat on the leather Chesterfield.

"I hated doing it, Chris. But I've tried as hard as I can to stay with my marriage. It was doomed from the moment we moved into the homestead with Ruth."

"Why didn't you move out?"

"And take Enid away from the place she adored? Then when Kyall came it was impossible. Ruth idolized the boy. She set him up as her heir. Kyall McQueen. Your mother and I were never a loving couple. In our early days I was very fond of her. We had an understanding. I suppose I thought or hoped it would work out. But both of us had made terrible choices and we had to be responsible for them. I could never have lost you children. And Ruth would have seen to it that I did."

"She'd have let me go like a shot." Christine laughed shortly.

"I don't think so. She needed you to torment. Your mother is just a born nagger."

"She's devastated," Christine said. "Slashed wide open."

Max's whole body winced. "I'm truly sorry, but I have

a right to some happiness in life. You and Kyall don't need me now. And your mother has never needed me."

"I don't think that's right at all, Dad. She just doesn't know how to show it."

"Don't you think that amounts to the same thing? It's all too late now. Ruth's death ended the whole sorry charade. I need to be my own man, not your mother's lackey. Anyway, for the first time in my life I'm deeply, truly in love."

And didn't she understand how glorious that was! "May I ask who she is?" Christine spoke gently.

"You don't know her. She came to the town after you left. She's very beautiful and very talented. A lot younger than I am, but nevertheless she loves me. Her name is Carol Lu. She's an artist. She paints landscapes and she gives classes. I thought she was unattainable—that the whole thing, the attraction, was in my mind—then all of a sudden I knew. She cares as much for me as I care for her. She gives me strength. The strength to make this clean break."

"But, Dad, it's like an amputation," Christine protested. "I know Mum isn't good at it, but she does love you. I don't think it has ever occurred to her you'd leave her."

"I am leaving her, Chris," her father said, "and I don't feel guilty. It's a tremendous experience for me, breaking up my marriage, but I'm sick to death of living a lie. For a long time now my marriage has been pointless and joyless. I don't want to die without experiencing some happiness. Carol can give it to me and I to her. We communicate in a way your mother and I never have. It's a wonderful, extraordinary intimacy. And I can't give it up. I can't take living here any more either."

Christine felt such a rush of gloom she actually slumped. "You can't mean you're leaving before Kyall's wedding, Dad? The timing couldn't be worse."

"Do you think I haven't thought of that?" Max bowed his head. "I never meant to speak out today, but something your mother said—something about my failing her—brought it all to a head. She simply doesn't know how to give relief or comfort. She never got any as a child and it scarred her for life."

"What's Kyall going to say?"

"Kyall won't be surprised," Max answered quietly, but with inner confidence. "Kyall won't begrudge me happiness either. I know this has come as a terrible wrenching shock to your mother, and to you, but this is my last chance at happiness and I'm going to seize it. The marriage is over."

In one way it would be a tremendous relief to get away to Sydney, Christine thought. As hard as she tried she couldn't meet her mother's needs, or help her deal with this deeply painful crisis in her life.

In her mother's eyes, and with her mother's talent for self-dramatization, Christine had become the enemy, not an ally. Christine had always loved her father the best. The two of them had always taken one another's side. Enid couldn't and wouldn't face the painful truth that she, with massive support from Ruth, had created her own problems—alienating her husband to the extent he was desperate to strike out in another direction with another woman who made him feel totally loved.

As her father had predicted, Kyall hadn't been shocked by the news. To him it had seemed inevitable, given the awesome power his grandmother had wielded over both his parents—keeping his mother tied close to the apron strings and at the same time treating his father as an outsider. Like Christine, he hated to see their mother in desperate pain, but neither could fail to feel sympathy for their father's plight.

It was a grievous situation, generating a lot of anger on Enid's part, and it had thrown the wedding plans into a quandary. Finally, after a series of family meetings, Max and Enid had agreed to maintain a united front—at least until after the wedding was over.

"I couldn't survive the shame," Enid had told them with burning black eyes.

Perhaps she secretly believed the marriage could be rebuilt. Neither Kyall nor Christine held out any such hopes.

Plans for the polo-picnic day were fast-tracked by Sarah, with Christine's valuable help, to fit in with Christine's schedule. The hospital always ran on a tight budget, despite the McQueens' legendary generosity. It was Christine's late grandmother who had caused the Bush Hospital to be built in the first place; in all honesty, it was one of the few truly good things the despotic Ruth had ever done.

With Sarah so busy at the hospital, and her mother so shaken by events, it fell to Christine to do much of the organizing—which suited her just fine. It kept her occupied and she found she had a natural flair for the job. Also, she loved the game of polo—polo being the focus of sporting activities in the Outback. There were other sports too, but exciting, potentially dangerous polo brought in the crowds and got the juices flowing. More to the point, as Sarah pointed out, it brought in donations for the hospital. The bigger the win of a favourite team, the bigger the donation.

Kyall's team, which included Mitch, was hot favourite to win. Both men were wonderful athletes. Kyall was now lost to his legions of female fans, as he was shortly to marry Sarah, but Mitch was still available. Most of them knew all about his long relationship with Christine Reardon, but the hot gossip was—and Christine couldn't seem to correct it—that she was involved with Ben Savage, who was due in Australia to promote his TV show. That left the gorgeous Mitch still out there, as far as all the local girls were concerned.

It turned out to be a wonderful day—a great success as a fundraiser, with everyone saying they must do it again.

The Logan sisters attended, as a matter of course, seated amid a large group of young people, all of them friends since childhood. Amanda, in character, looked very eye-catching—teasing, posing, laughing impishly, letting out little screams of excitement when Mitch in particular thundered down the field, her big blue eyes openly devouring him. She was determined on having a good time, which apparently included flirting with every attractive man in sight despite her enormous crush on Mitchell Claydon. For Amanda, flirting appeared to be second nature.

Afterwards Amanda made it her business to track down Mitch who, as a member of the winning team, looked like a god in the saddle and was surrounded by admirers, male and female. Everyone knew Mitch. He was a great guy.

Amanda oozed her way in close, grabbing him by the arm. "Aren't you going to say hello to an old friend?" She smiled brightly, hugging him so her breasts pressed into his arm.

"Hi, Amanda!" Mitch tossed her a casual smile. "You look very pretty." Indeed she did, with creamy bosoms popping out of a summery yellow halter-necked dress.

She let out a little squeal and twirled around. "I've never forgotten how you told me I looked good in yellow."

"You do," Mitch assured her in a somewhat less indulgent voice.

"Congratulations on your win," she said sweetly, feeling tingly all over.

"It was a great match. Shelley here with you?"

"Yes. We wouldn't have missed today for the world. When is Christine going back to Sydney?" she asked, willing the stunning, vivacious Christine, who was circling the guests, to stay away.

"Why don't you ask her?"

"I will." She laughed, a little bit of acid etched into the tinkle. "I must tell you how sorry I am I caused friction between you two. I was certain I'd read that article, but it must have been about someone else."

"Forget it, Amanda. I have. Just be more careful in future."

"Oh, I will. I felt just dreadful afterwards. Naturally I apologised to Christine. She's such a lovely person and she understood. These things happen all the time."

"What things?" Mitch looked over Amanda's head with its buttery curls.

He could see Christine in the near distance, her lovely thick, springy hair, worn loose the way he liked it, lifting in the breeze. She looked effortlessly, supremely elegant in an all-white outfit that showed off her beautiful body. She wore a slinky designer top with a blue and silver logo and narrow linen pants. She had done a great job of organizing this event, and was a vibrant presence in the swarming sea of faces. Chris was very good with people. She made everything come right. But he couldn't wait to get her to himself.

"You know the way things get misreported." Amanda was nattering away like a flea in his ear. "But I didn't get this wrong." In a flash she unzipped her yellow shoulder bag, pulling out a folded piece of newspaper and waving it tauntingly like a red flag at a bull. "Didn't Christine tell us her affair with Ben Savage was well and truly over?"

"Amanda, don't embarrass yourself," Mitch warned, but Amanda fumbled with the newspaper as the breeze threatened to whip it from her and shoved it beneath his nose.

"So what's that, then?" She looked up at Mitch triumphantly, stabbing a fingernail at the clipping so hard it tore. "A red-hot example of lust, or is it love?"

"Throw it away, Amanda," Mitch advised coolly. "That's an old picture. It says so right there."

"Sure, but you have to admit that's some smooch!"

Anger engulfed him. "What do you hope to gain by this, Amanda?"

She seized his hand, looking up at him earnestly. "I'm on your side, Mitch. I'm your friend. I'm here for you. I want to save you pain."

"You're way too kind."

"I really care about you, Mitch," she protested. "When I saw that picture in the paper it worried me deeply. How can anyone turn it on and off so easily? Especially with that guy. Let's face it. She left you once. She'll do it again."

"I'd like to think that's my business, Amanda, not yours." Mitch looked at her directly. "Why don't you toddle off now? I'd be more than grateful."

"Oh, Mitch, you make me sound like a troublemaker..."

"Amanda, we already know you are."

What a meddlesome little bitch, Mitch thought as, lip trembling, Amanda flounced off. But she was right about one thing. That kiss looked very real. So real he was back to his fluctuating moods. Was it possible he and Ben Savage were united by one thing? Were both of them Christine's victims? Sometimes it seemed there was no reassurance to be had.

Trust me. That's all I'm asking you to do.

He could hear Christine's voice distinctly as it sounded in his head. He could see her large, beautiful eyes, imploring him to have faith in her. It should be easy. In some ways it was. But there was always something to stir up doubt.

Christine was still surrounded by people when Mitch joined her admiring group. Everything was good and pleasant; people were making jokes. She looked quickly at him and put out her hand, a slight look of puzzlement in her eyes as she tried to gauge his mood. He should have been in high spirits after his exciting win, but her long experience of him told her he wasn't.

"Excuse us, won't you?" She glanced around with a smile.

"Good show, Mitch." One of the spectators, a prominent grazier and an ex-champion polo player with a rock-hard physique, reached out and punched Mitch's shoulder. "That was one helluva game!"

"Thank you, sir."

"You and Kyall are really special."

"That's quite a compliment coming from you, sir."

"Never been more sincere in my life. Good luck to you, Mitch. Remember me to your father."

"Will do."

"Is something wrong?" Christine asked as they moved away from the tented area where most of the guests were congregated, enjoying refreshments.

"No, not at all." Blue gums dripped dry leaves like confetti. They burnished her hair. He looked away. She tore his heart.

"Your eyes tend to give you away Mitch" she said gently.

"So I've been told."

"I suspect bouncy little Amanda might have something to do with it. I spotted you talking to her."

"No, you spotted her talking to me," he corrected.

"So what did she say this time to get under your skin?"

"You should stop asking those kind of questions, Chris."

"No, you should answer. That's if we want a future together—"

"Dare I hope?" he cut in sardonically.

"Do you want to hope? That's the point. There's no one else, Mitch."

"Honest?" He gave her a half-smile though he wanted to cry out, I love you. But still he couldn't.

"Don't be difficult," she begged. "It's been such a good day. I haven't spoken to a single person who isn't delighted to be here."

"It's quite a crowd." He looked about. The bunting and the women's dresses were an explosion of colour in the hot sun.

"You need a crowd at a fundraiser. I'm pleased because this is my first."

"You've done an excellent job." It made him a little ashamed he couldn't sound more enthusiastic—he *was* very proud of her.

"You're making me feel uncomfortable, Mitch," she said, dodging another cascade of falling leaves. "What did Amanda say to you? Obviously she's lurking in the wings, hoping I'll disappear from your life."

"Again?"

"You're being a bastard, really." She caught his hand, instantly raising tingles. "Why are you feeling so threatened? I thought we'd worked that out."

He stared down at their joined hands. Hers so smooth, soft-skinned and white, his deeply tanned, hardened from his way of life. "If you look at this thing coldly, Chrissy, I don't really know your plans. You tell me you're thinking positively of ditching your career. I'd love to believe it. But anything could happen when you get back to Sydney. All the razzle-dazzle will start up again. You'll have a job on your hands just fending Savage off.''

"Okay." She raised her chin, her voice low and tight. "So this is all connected to Ben? Little screwball Amanda is passing on a lot of information. I thought I'd warned her.''

He made no immediate answer, keeping hold of her hand. "I don't take any notice of Amanda, Chrissy. I think my own deep thoughts.''

"But you can't push away the past?''

He felt a powerful tide of love towards her. "I've told you before. It's not an easy thing for anyone to do. On the other hand, a future without you is just too bleak to contemplate.''

"You think I wouldn't suffer too?''

His hand tightened unconsciously, causing her to give an involuntary little whimper. "I'm sorry," he apologized immediately, easing his grip on her, "but that kind of thing only raises expectations. Be careful with that.''

"I mean what I say, Mitch. You can't keep punishing me. We have to move on.''

"I know." He stopped walking so he could turn to look at her, wanting desperately to kiss her, to feel her slender, pliant body in his arms. The longing was so unbearable sometimes he felt a kind of contempt for his own weakness.

To crush her mouth! He looked down at it. It was like a full-blown rose. He wanted to crumple it with the weight of his kiss. Impossible at the moment, with so many people about. But this was Christine, the sweet, ardent, beautiful long-legged creature he had loved from boyhood. He loved her more than his own life, of course. That was his trouble. He was unchanged and unchangeable.

"If I follow you to Sydney and you let me do that, I'll never let you go," he warned. "You're the woman I want. One day mother of my kids. You're my life. That's a big responsibility, Chrissy. You'd better think long and hard."

"Can't you believe I've been doing just that?" she whispered, feeling so tender towards him she wanted to fold him into the softness of her breasts.

Despite the people around them, he couldn't help but put his arm around her waist. "I don't want you to leave." The dappled sun gilded his face and struck pure gold from his hair. "Not for a minute. I want you beside me every morning I wake, the first face I see. Every night I want to make love to you in our bed. Nobody but you. It might be a strain, knowing that."

Tears glittered like jewels in her eyes and she didn't bother to hide them. "But I want that too, Mitch, more than anything in life."

"You do now." He let his gaze rest on her beautiful face. "But you're going away very soon. Tell me again after you go back to Sydney."

CHAPTER NINE

THE fashion critics and the fashion spectators loved the parades.

"Christine Reardon isn't a supermodel for nothing," the editor of one high-profile style magazine was quoted as saying.

She was a great success—an international model but one of their own.

Much was made of the fact she glowed with health and vitality, because the eating disorder anorexia was causing grave concern around the world and within sections of the industry itself. For all models, dieting was a way of life. Some of her friends in the business near starved to maintain their so skinny bodies, but she made sure she kept to a healthy diet and an exercise program worked out for her by an expert who'd helped shape a lot more famous bodies than her own. It took effort and discipline, but it worked, leaving her with a figure that drew "wow's"!

After the final parade—though she still had a swimsuit promotion to do—everyone piled into limousines, heading off for a party and buffet at a top society hostess's opulent harbourside mansion. It was post-parade mania as usual.

She wore one of the evening's show-stoppers, a beaded silk chiffon gown in deep turquoise and purple, and a collection of turquoise and sterling silver bracelets on her arms, the elaborate matching pendant earrings swinging like chandeliers from her ears. She was expected to look very glamorous and sexy, which meant just that bit over the top, but it was all harmless enough.

What wasn't so harmless was the fact Ben Savage kept turning up everywhere she went, promoting the public perception they were still a hot item. How would Mitch feel if this ever got back to him? There were no guarantees she wasn't being watched by some private investigator. After that business with Amanda Logan nothing would surprise her. But Ben was on a high. His trip to Oz was a phenomenal success. He was everywhere in Sydney—on talk shows, at parties, functions, shopping centres.

True to his promise, he had attended tonight's parade, where a plethora of females had vied in embarrassing fashion for his attention. But he had persisted in staring up at Christine on the catwalk as though she was the sexiest woman in the world. He'd already tried to sweep her into one of those Californian clinches he'd perfected on his afternoon soap, but she'd elbowed him in the ribs.

Maybe it was going to take a little time for their split to sink in.

An hour or so later, at the party, he tried to kiss her again. She was tempted to tell him she was madly, deeply and truly in love with someone else, but she thought it might feed his competitiveness. That was the thing. Most actors were very competitive.

Around two a.m. she decided she just had to make her getaway. She'd held up just fine—she and Ben were the life of the party, which was precisely what their hostess expected—but her *joie de vivre* didn't stretch to three a.m.

She was quietly trying to ring herself a cab when Ben appeared at her elbow.

"You're so lucky, darlin'. A limousine awaits."

"Really? A limousine?" Christine wasn't sure if he was telling the truth or not.

"Honey, would I lie to you?"

"Yes, you would."

"Okay, then…" Ben turned, his eyes alighting on their very soignée hostess. "Can I talk to you, Jessy, please?"

Jessica Kimball who never, but never, answered to Jessy, cruised to their side. "Anything, Ben." She looked up at him with mischief in her eyes.

"Could you please tell Christine here that there's a limousine at her disposal?"

Jessica hid her disappointment. "But of course, Christine. Surely you're not leaving? This lot are going to party all night."

"I haven't had much sleep this past week, Jessica," Christine apologized. "But I do thank you for a marvellous evening."

"Our pleasure. You and Ben are a wonderful double act. You're not going too, Ben?"

"I just can't let her leave alone, Jessy."

"I understand." Jessica's smile was arch. "But you've both got to promise you'll come to the little reception I'm giving next week."

"You couldn't keep us away!" Ben bent gallantly to kiss Jessica Kimball's cheek.

"So, where to?" Ben asked when they were tucked into the back seat of the luxurious limo. So far he hadn't been able to find out where Chris was staying. That was top secret.

Christine gave him the address, a twenty-minute drive away.

"About time too," said Ben, the super-optimist, with unwarranted satisfaction.

Mitch had heard about how great a fashion model Christine was. He'd even studied her photographs on the quiet—photos that appeared in the fashion magazines his mother subscribed to. Now he was seeing her in action. She was extravagantly beautiful with her flawless hair and make-up. Her clothes were a treasure trove of evening gear, featuring the most beautiful colours and fabrics he'd ever seen in his life. Already tall she was a goddess in high-heeled sandals. How she didn't stumble and break her neck he'd never know. In fact he was fearful, but there she was, stepping it out—sometimes darn near at a gallop—with all the in-built confidence and panache of a creation who hardly seemed to touch the ground.

His Chrissy! Boy, was he in deep! The very sight of her melted his bones.

He was lucky to have found a seat. The parade was a sell-out. But a very pleasant older woman, whose face seemed way too small for her incredible hairdo, had shown she had clout by fitting him in towards the rear of the huge room. That didn't bother him at all. He was here to surprise Chris as well as get a chance to see her strut her stuff, and sure enough she was marvelous, with some technique of moving and showing off the clothes that the other models, despite their good looks and good figures, couldn't match. Small wonder she had made it in this business. She had everything!

Looking around him, he could see that people loved her. She smiled at them. Really smiled. She looked vivid and vital. She looked as if she loved her audience and they embraced her.

Which was precisely what he desperately wanted to do. These intervening weeks had been a tough time for him. He had delivered his ultimatum and even now he wasn't sure if Chris was truly ready to sacrifice what must be a glamorous life. Now there was a great waiting. A kind of suspended animation until he was face to face with her again and could hear her say those three little words he so desperately wanted and needed to hear. I love you.

Ten minutes later, as she was showing off a seductive midnight-blue lace gown—what size was her tiny waist?—he spotted the American soap star, his *doppelgänger*, Ben Savage.

Wasn't that just lovely! Shock quickly crystallized into a rush of hostility the like of which Mitch had never experienced before. The reason why he hadn't spotted Savage before—and God knows he'd looked—was that Savage had for some reason changed places with a big burly guy who would have looked more at home driving an armoured van. It was impossible to miss his resemblance to himself. Savage might have been a Claydon. He was sitting down, so he didn't know how tall Savage was, but he sure stood out from the crowd.

After that his sense of enthrallment went rapidly downhill. The rest of the parade was painful to endure. He spent as much time watching Savage and his reactions—which the soap star made no effort to hide—as Christine. Savage, bless him, was very, very supportive. His eyes were glued to Christine's every appearance which he greeted with applause, picking up his conversations with the other guests immediately she moved off-stage.

So Savage was still very much taken with Chris. Maybe that was why he was here in Australia? Wasn't it a long way to come to promote a soap opera? Maybe Savage had decided to ask Chris to marry him? What he was witnessing wasn't smiling affection for an ex-girlfriend. It was an intimate reaction. God knows, they'd been lovers. If that wasn't enough to inspire animosity, what was?

The talk at his table was all about the gala post-parade party at the home of some very well heeled society hostess—Jessica something. The woman beside him—Heather—had already told him with effusive gaiety she thought she'd been seeing double when he'd arrived.

"Why, you and Ben are so alike you could be brothers!"

Sacred cow! He'd hoped she would tell him more about the "fabulous" post-parade party; instead she issued an invitation of her own.

"Listen, I have the most marvellous idea. Why don't you join us? We're going on to a nightclub."

He'd regretfully declined, citing a previous engagement, trying to be pleasant when he was feeling jangled beyond belief.

Christine and Savage. He definitely wanted an explanation.

When he finally made it backstage there was such a packed gathering it was difficult to move. Someone actually called him Mr Savage along the way, albeit uncertainly, causing him to grind his teeth. And instead of being there in all her glory, Christine, he was told, had been whisked off in a limousine. Naturally Ben Savage had been one of the party. Were they related?

He'd had more than enough of that.

He had no idea when she'd be back. But he did know where she was staying. Kyall had told him about the apartment he'd bought in Sydney for his and the family's use. It was bound to be an up-market pad. Kyall did a lot of travelling on family business, and an apartment suited him better than a hotel. Chris, in fact, would be the first one to make use of it.

Chris? Or Chris and the soap star? The thought that Chris mightn't be one hundred per cent faithful might drive him insane. As it was he was in turmoil. He had the appalling notion that Christine and Savage might be back together again. These things, however repellent, happened. There was always the possibility Christine's affections for him hadn't proved strong enough.

What an agony! He was sickened by his own feelings of

insecurity. Surely if he loved her he shouldn't be so ready
to pre-judge? Surely he owed her the chance to explain.

It had better be good!

The penthouse apartment had a phenomenal view. He
might have known. It was a wide-angled one that took in
sparkling Rushcutter's Bay, its beautiful marina afloat with
all manner of craft and the occasional mega-yacht. There
was a long view of the Sydney Opera House, with its famous billowing white "sails" lit to night-time radiance,
and just behind it the noble span of the Sydney Harbour
Bridge, one of the longest and certainly the widest steel-
arch bridge in the world.

It and the Opera House identified Sydney for all
Australians and visitors from all over the world. He
couldn't think of another harbour more blue or more magnificent. And over the years he had managed to see them
all. The city's night-time glitter was spectacular too.

While he was here he'd intended to hit the beaches with
Chris. Sydney's thirteen beaches, between Manly and Palm
Beach, were among the best in the world. The restaurants
weren't bad either, catering for every conceivable taste and
culture. This was a big, cosmopolitan city. Another big plus
for him was the warm, fine weather. Summer was much
milder than in his fiery desert home.

He turned away from the view to inspect the apartment.
Kyall had given him a key in case Chris wasn't available
to meet him when he arrived. She had a tight schedule.
Kyall must have been working with someone—an interior
designer—because Mitch found as he wandered around the
easy-flowing layout that the apartment had been fully fur-
nished: not with the traditional grandeur of Wunnamurra's
legendary homestead, but with a more contemporary tai-
lored look, bringing in a lot of comfort and luxury.

He approved of the beautiful wood floors and the designer rugs. The sofas and the armchairs in the living room
weren't too bad either. They offered a lot of comfort. And
wasn't comfort what he needed?

He made himself a stiff drink, Scotch on the rocks, before sinking into a deep armchair, facing the sparkling
view, and loosening his tie. The idea was to catch forty
winks—he'd been endlessly on the go just to get here—
before Chris arrived home.

On her own? A feeling of dread stuck in his throat.

He'd had a truly terrible time after Chris had run off that
first time. It had never left his consciousness. Her absence
had never cured him. He took a swallow of his Scotch—
the best; the McQueens knew how to live—unwilling to
allow those old feelings of loss and rejection to creep over
him again. If she had Savage by her side he honestly
couldn't condone the guy's getting through the door. He'd
heave himself to his feet and mosey on home to Marjimba,
leaving the situation wide open to his rival.

If he couldn't trust Chris it made no sense to marry her.
The risk she would run again was too high. He saw clearly
he mightn't let her do it.

Ben insisted on coming up to her door. Christine knew
there wasn't a small part of him that would represent a
threat to her, but he literally wouldn't go away. He wanted
to have his say before he left the city. It was clear he genuinely thought giving up her glittering career, which she
had hinted at, was one big mistake.

At her door he touched her shoulder lightly. "One for
the road?"

"I'd rather we didn't, Ben."

"You know you can trust me."

"I do trust you, Ben. You're what my mother calls a gentleman."

"What do you call me?"

"A good friend."

"Then let me in for a few moments, Chris," he begged, with a little-boy-lost look Mitch definitely didn't have. "If I could wrap my arms around you it would take away the pain. We should never have parted."

"We did, Ben, remember? And you've had quite a few affairs in between. So this isn't a great idea."

He gave her a long, almost uncomprehending look. "It makes no difference if I tell you I still love you?"

"Ben, our affair is behind us. It was good fun, but it couldn't last."

"That was my stupid fault." He dropped his head onto her shoulder, giving her the curious notion he'd done that very thing in his soap. "We were great together. How about one kiss before I go?"

"I'd sooner not lead you into temptation." She couldn't help smiling.

"One weeniest little kiss for old times' sake?"

"No."

"No? Once it used to be yes." He straightened, taking her face tenderly in his hands. "Short and sweet?" But he just couldn't keep to it, for all his honest intentions.

Mitch came out of a light drowse to hear voices at the door. Chris, unmistakably, and a man with a very definite American accent. Ben Savage. He had an eerie feeling of heightened awareness. The big question was: would Christine dismiss Savage at the door?

Several moments elapsed and they were still out there, but doing what? Mitch intended to find out. Savage was obviously as obsessively in love with Christine as he was. He stood up purposefully, raking a hand through his hair as he walked to the foyer. He didn't particularly want to startle Chris, even if she was living on the edge in a promiscuous kind of life. He didn't mind giving Savage a fright though.

God, was that a moan? If she was moaning, with all that entailed, things would never be the same.

Feeling no guilt at all, Mitch threw open the door, catching the two people outside—man and woman locked in a passionate embrace.

He was so angry it might come to violence. "At least I now know you two *are* an item," he said in a voice so cold it appeared to affect Savage more than any seething rage.

"Mitch!" Christine broke away. In her sapphire eyes he saw a painful mix of embarrassment and—incredibly— pleasure to see him.

How bizarre! "Chrissy, darling, how are you? There are just no words to describe how I feel at this moment."

Christine felt the icy chill. It swept from her ankles to her head. "Kyall gave you a key?"

"He's nothing if not my best friend. And you're Ben, of course. I'm absolutely riveted by our resemblance."

"Do you know? So am I." Ben stared at him. "So you're Chris's Mitch. I've heard so much about you." Ben, the experienced actor, found a charming smile even when he was seriously panicked. This guy looked like one tough Aussie.

"Oh? What have you heard?" Mitch glanced from one to the other, eyes glittering.

Christine quickly put herself between the two men. Mitch was taller, rangier, with a steel in him she knew Ben the playboy didn't have. Side by side there were very marked differences. "Ben was just saying goodnight, Mitch."

"Yes, time to go." Ben felt incredibly awkward, but tried hard to keep it all together. He wasn't looking for a fight. Not with this guy. "Great to meet you, Mitch. You're a lucky man. Keep in touch, Chris." He blew her a kiss as he hotfooted it away.

"Thanks for bringing me home, Ben."

"A pleasure. Be good." Ben made such a dash for the lift one would have thought Mitch was in hot pursuit. Mercifully for all, it was already at the top floor. He disappeared with another quick wave of his hand.

"I thought you had to be sixteen to leave a man with a kiss outside the door," Mitch said in a hard, judgmental voice. "I was waiting for you to invite him in."

"Hey, he was leaving." Christine feared an explosion of tension.

"Just a bit embarrassing, don't you think?" He was angry, though fierce splinters of desire pressed into his flesh.

"You weren't supposed to be here for a couple of days." She tried to head him off.

"As it turns out it was a good time to catch you out."

"Catch me out? Oh, really!" She spun on her heel, her long silk chiffon skirt floating around her legs.

"Well, didn't I?" He followed her, turbulence, anger, desire all mixed up together. There were too many disturbing memories in his mind.

"Ben was kissing me goodbye."

"I didn't think he was giving you mouth to mouth resuscitation. It's a bit rich, inviting me here, Chrissy, keeping me forever on a string, while you have Savage on the side."

"Except that's not the case," she said fierily. "I love you."

"Yeah! I remember you said that once before." He didn't hide his disgust. "You're just sowing all your wild oats before you get married?"

Her beautiful hair had such volume it framed her face like a thick cloud. "Look, Ben and I were over ages ago. I still like him. He's still my friend."

"And it's normal to have sex with your friends?" Bitter disillusionment consumed him.

"Mitch, I really do think your jealousy has you unhinged."

"Absolutely." He gave a brief laugh. "I don't like your giving Savage the green light. Not when you'd convinced me you were ready to settle down."

"For God's sake, Mitch, I wasn't committing adultery!" Her own voice turned hard. "It was just a kiss."

"If only I could swallow that. Sorry, Chrissy, I can't. It looked terribly involved." He swung away from her. Her beautiful face, her beautiful body. Those were a woman's weapons.

"What are you doing?" She rushed after him, grabbing his sleeve.

"I'm going. It's my turn to do a runner."

After all this time he'd still never forgive her. "Please don't go, Mitch," she begged. "Please. We can get past this. It's nothing."

"I'm sorry." He shook her off. "I prefer faithful women."

"While you've had relationships with at least half a dozen women since I've been gone," she countered with some tartness. "What about that little vixen, Amanda Logan?"

"Spoken by the woman who thinks nothing of two-timing me."

"Aren't you just leaping to conclusions? Surely you don't really think I wanted Ben to kiss me?"

"You were fighting him off, right?"

"He just got carried away."

"That's for sure." Mitch didn't attempt to hide his contempt.

"I love you, Mitch. Can't you get it through your thick head?"

"Apparently not." He gave her a little push away from him, furious he still wanted her so badly.

"Ben would have been upset if we hadn't parted friends."

"God!" He exploded. "Cut it out! I bet he's been kissing you the whole bloody time he's been here."

"Mitch—please." She couldn't mishandle this one. "Just because Ben got carried away tonight, it doesn't mean I did."

"You were just pretending to like it? Could you please take your hand off my arm?"

"No." She met the blue dazzle of his eyes. "You owe it to me to calm down and listen."

"It's not like that, Chrissy." Almost gently he removed her hand. "I owe you nothing."

"So, it's very much a conditional love?" She stared at him with burning intensity.

"I haven't got your capacity for sharing."

"You know your trouble, Mitch? You're emotionally damaged."

"I may finally be over it.

The resolution in his face put her in turmoil. She flew after him as he stalked to the door. "Why are we fighting? I wasn't counting on anything like this."

"Is that supposed to make me feel better?"

"I love you, Mitch," she said emotionally, clinging to his back. "I can't see life without you."

"Stop that." God, he couldn't bear it. The lies, the longing. It tortured him.

"Stop what? This is all a horrible mistake." She locked her arms around him. "Please don't do this, Mitch. I love you. We can't destroy what we've got."

That was when he started going crazy. He was obsessively in love with her—drawn by her beauty and charisma since they were kids together. But surely the insanity had to end? Tonight he had intended to ask her to marry him. He had the engagement ring in his breast pocket. He could feel it press against his heart.

"Let go, Chris!" Eerily, her trying to hold onto him heightened the intoxication.

"No, not when we have a chance." She threw up her head, her eyes a smouldering sapphire-blue. The exact colour of the central precious stone in the ring he'd intended to give her.

"Why pretend, Chris? What's the point of it? You can't really explain why Savage was here. I was at the parade tonight—"

"You weren't! Why didn't you come backstage to see me? I'd have been thrilled."

Something in her voice caught him off-guard. The unmistakable ring of truth. "I did come backstage, as it happens. But you and Savage had already left for the party."

"You could have followed. You're a friend of mine—"

"A *friend*?" he exploded. "I had dreams, Christine. You ruined them."

"Which is the more powerful emotion, Mitch? Love or jealousy?"

"I would have to say, in my case, jealousy. I'm not

proud of it, but there you are. Would you mind taking your long, pretty fingers off my arm?''

''No, I won't. You have to see sense. You're as stubborn as a mule. You always were. But we have to talk about this, Mitch.''

''We can't. I'm not a complete fool. You and Savage are lovers. If I hadn't suddenly appeared he'd be in your bed by now.''

''Go on—do what you do best!'' She launched at him, striking his chest with her fist. ''Damage our lives. I don't need that look of disgust either. You're just plain paranoid. Ben and I had a relationship—it had a lot to do with his resemblance to you—''

''Kinky, wouldn't you say?'' He caught her wrist and held it.

''Probably. I used to imagine he was you, which was terribly unfair to Ben. We split up. There was nothing deep to sustain us. I always wanted to come home.''

''Forget all that!'' he warned. ''I saw Savage looking at you. I saw the way he was kissing you. It's far from over with him.''

''Who cares? Ben has a tendency to want the woman he can't get.''

''Hell, you don't have to explain something like that to me. You were going to give yourself to Savage and we both know it.''

''Give him a kiss? Yes, damn it, I was. Is that what you want me to say?''

All of a sudden she was crying, while he stood there, his anger turning to shock and dismay. Chris had never cried— even when she took nasty spills. ''Chris?'' he said tentatively.

''Shut up. I've had just about enough of you, Mitch Claydon.'' She spun away as her tears started to flow in earnest. "What compels you to distrust me? Is it ever going to end? So it was unfortunate Ben was here. Sometimes he's unstoppable, but he's harmless. I tell you I love you, but that's not enough. You want to keep at it and at it. I never knew you were so cruel."

"I guess I must be." He was astonished at the intensity and the nature of his warring emotions. Why, in his dealings with Christine, was there always this mad reversal? He was recoiling even as he wanted to comfort her, to take her into his arms and kiss her tears away. He couldn't begin to understand the depth and power of her hold over him.

In her effort to distance herself from him Christine caught her high heel in the hem of her beautiful deep turquoise gown.

"Damn, damn, damn!" She struggled to free it, the pendant earrings she wore swinging wildly against her heated cheeks.

"Chris—let me."

"Go away," she flashed. "Go back to Marjimba and that devious little Amanda."

"Sorry. I can't." He managed to lay a hand on her bare, silky shoulder, but she tore away furiously, keeping her face averted so he wouldn't see her tears.

It wasn't something he could explain to himself. It just was. He went after her, hauling her into his arms. She wouldn't let him hold her but he did all the same, easily subduing her struggles though she was strong and athletic.

"Steady, steady!" He might have been talking to a high-spirited filly.

"Go to hell!"

"Without you, I'm there." He pressed her body in the beautiful dress to him.

Immediately he was trapped by desire, urgent cravings, aware she was trembling and yet unable to disguise their magnetic attraction. She tilted her body back slightly, looking up at him with passionate defiance in her eyes. "Go ahead. Give way to your anger. I give you permission."

"To do what?" He moved his hand up to her slender nape, hidden beneath her wealth of hair. He clutched it, holding her face to him.

"Do what you like. I don't give a damn!"

"I think I might get that dress off you first."

She made no response, though her breathing picked up dramatically. He could see the rise and fall of her perfect deep breasts through the sheer material. "I swear to you, Mitch—"

"Go ahead." She was so beautiful it blinded him. Her hair was like a dark, wind-tossed storm around her face. He bent his head so his mouth captured hers. The pleasure was so voluptuous it loosened his knees. Her mouth had a distinctive taste, like citrus and honey.

Here was the precipice. He had a choice. He could jump or step back. Only he might as well be lost in a bottomless abyss as live without Chris. The touch of her mouth, the play of her tongue filled him with leaping desire.

"I love you." Slowly, as though she was very unsure of what he might do, she lifted her hands to hold his face. "You've always been that special, unforgettable person in my life."

"So special you forgot all about me!" His single dimple flicked in and out with self-derision. "But you won't forget this time, my love!"

He'd made the choice. Now he jumped. His heart rose up into his throat, his veins saturated with the heat of passion. This was the way it always was with Chris.

Could women cast a spell? Yes. Yes. Yes.

He made her drop her hands while his mouth moved slowly, lingeringly, down over the so smooth skin of her face to the centre of his longing—her deep rose mouth, so plush and seductive. It was astonishing, his hunger for her. What was her price? Sapphires, diamonds, rubies, pearls? She was above them all.

He kissed her until she couldn't stand, until she didn't know what she was doing or saying. He felt the answering excitement rage through her as she willingly assuaged the furious frustration and desire that was in him.

For her height she was a lightweight. He had no trouble lifting her, carrying her down to the main bedroom he already knew she was occupying.

Lying on top the silver-blue quilt, he studied her, this extraordinarily beautiful young woman.

"Chrissy, I'm going to make love to you." It was the most inevitable thing in the world.

The bedside lamps caught the bright golden sheen of his hair, his sea-blue eyes, the tension in him. "I want you to," she said, clearly displaying the depth of her emotions. "Hold nothing back."

"I don't want you to talk either."

"Because I might say the wrong thing?"

"There's no room for words." Intently he found the long hidden zipper of her dress, pulling it down over her breasts. Her upper torso was immediately naked—she wore no bra—as he slid the exquisite gown down over her taut stomach, then down over her hips, the long lovely length of her legs. Everything in slow motion. Everything with care, while she shifted her body to allow the dress to come away from her.

With the bedside lamps turned full on her she was perfection, her extended arms making stroking motions over the smooth shining surface of the coverlet. It struck him as incredibly erotic, increasing the level of longing that threatened to overcome him. His hand found the narrow ribbed band at the top of her blue satin briefs. She quivered in anticipation, taut as a bow.

Neither of them spoke.

When she was naked he stood and began removing his own clothes, his strong arms trembling when she rose from the bed and came behind him, laying her face against the bare skin of his back. As he had helped her, so she began to help him undress, the taut passion in their faces clearly visible.

"What I feel for you will never change." He turned to her, his mouth descending along her neck to her breast, the nipple erect, just as he wanted it. He could feel all the little jumping nerves, the muscles in her tight buttocks as he pressed her naked body to his. Her lovely long legs parted, gloriously yielding, as his hands moved over her.

"Could I make you pregnant?"

She felt like laughing madly, headily, in delight. "It's possible—but you should have made me pregnant long ago." Emotion so stirred her body she felt it like an expanding force.

He drew back to stare down at her. "No regrets?"

She clutched at him. "I thought we weren't going to talk?" Her eyes blazed, invited, challenged.

"Come to me now and I'll never let you go," he warned, even then feeling the panic of losing her.

"When are you going to understand, Mitch? I love you. Only you," she said very seriously, touching his mouth with delicate fingers. "Lay down all your fears. They're unfounded. I'm home to stay." She raised her arms, all woman.

He picked her up, his tenderness grown a little fierce. The roar in his heart was like the roar of a lion.

He issued himself a stern order: let go of the rage and the heartbreak of the past. The old dreams that didn't come true. All his doubts had to stop if they were to make up for lost time. Suffering might even have been necessary in order to feel this incredible rapture. There seemed no limit to it. He would never allow her to forget her promise. It had restored him.

Mitch laid her on the bed, cascades of dark silky hair sliding all over the pillows and cushions. He turned her beautiful body this way and that, so fluid, so satiny soft, while he stripped off the silver-blue coverlet.

Finally he levered himself over her, glorying in her naked body beneath him, tantalising her, so desiring, so easy to arouse—withholding his manhood though she gave little cries of entreaty. He wasn't ready to enter her until he'd given her as much pleasure as she gave him.

The more he gave her, the more she wanted. She unfolded her whole body to his hands and his mouth. She was woman. His mate. She wound herself around him, whispering endearments. The sheet got all tangled and he threw it away. She climbed over him. Fell on him. He withstood the ravishing torment as long as he could, rotating her luscious body, his hands at her waist, spanning it, while she arced up and down.

Enough! He was fully aroused. He spun her like a ballerina onto her back, groaning with unparalleled sensations. His blood was exploding with a million fiery sparks.

"W-wait!" Her voice was low, shaken, yet incredibly erotic. "I'll t-tell you."

He forced himself to hold back for the briefest of white-hot moments, until they were moving rhythmically together, perfect partners in a love dance. It was unbearable, but then it was glorious. His strong heart was fluttering. She was denying him nothing. He knew a moment's shame for ever having doubted her.

"My beautiful Chris!"

He couldn't hold back a millisecond longer. His hunger was devouring him. He sank into her, plunged deeper and deeper, feeling her open and welcome him, her body closing on him, holding him exquisitely tight. Such pleasure was almost an agony, and his heart lurched and his head spun.

Finally she bucked against the mighty force of his impending orgasm, herself on the verge—coming...coming... He was so attuned to her he was listening for it as he would listen for a signal.

The flare of excitement was so powerful she wanted it to last forever. The flames shot higher and higher. Enduring flames that had never gone out. They were like one body, one mind. They shared the same intense hunger. Her breathing became ragged as she simply gave herself up to bliss.

Those high little keening cries were her own, she realized dazedly.

Sweat sizzled off her hot skin. She was circling higher and higher. Right into the eye of the sun. She was melting, insubstantial...

"Oh, yes!" The words burst from her in ecstasy.

He needed no second entreaty. His own momentum, muscular and powerfully strong, carried them into a new dimension of bright radiance where all needs and hungers were satisfied and all conflicts were laid to rest.

Separated in the past, they would never be parted again.

EPILOGUE

FROM the open French doors Christine could see the wedding guests moving all over the wide green lawns. There was a gentle breeze blowing in from the desert, muting the effects of the hot Outback sun. It fluttered the women's skirts so they looked like brightly coloured ribbons. Manicured hands reached up to anchor expensive wide-brimmed hats in a range of colours, decorations and styles, lest they be caught by the wind. The home gardens, watered by bores, were in full fragrant bloom, coaxed along by a team of gardeners so everything would be perfect for this very special day.

From where she looked out Christine could see the huge white marquees that had been set up in the grounds, the great shade trees lending additional protection. Everything was as beautiful as promised. This was Kyall's and Sarah's wedding day. The communion of two beautiful people. Two people she loved.

Love was moving inside her like a sensation of heavenly light. Since she and Mitch had become engaged she felt as if she'd been reborn. On a spontaneous impulse she lifted her ring to her mouth and kissed it.

It was so very, very beautiful—a symbol of their love, a glorious square-cut sapphire flanked by diamonds. Mitch had given it to her that very special night, when the two of them had made their decision to be together forever.

She knew in committing to Mitch she was doing the right thing. She had no qualms about turning her back on her career. There were no words to describe the great joy, the sense of security, the vision, that had come with that choice.

Christine Reardon, twenty-eight, now wanted with every particle of her being not to be a supermodel, but a wife and mother and a full partner in their marriage.

They planned to have four children. They could afford them. No decision could have been easier. Mitch professed in triumph to being the luckiest guy in the world, and in a few short months they too would be married. It would be her wedding day, and if possible she would be even happier than she was on this wonderful day.

She'd already begun to make plans: daydreaming about her wedding gown and veil, the favourite designer who would make it, what her bridesmaids would wear, the colours, the ceremony—she thought a temple in the garden—the reception, the food they would eat. But first she and Mitch would have to give all these guests time to recover from this day of days.

"Chris? What are you doing?"

A young excited voice called from outside the door.

"It's open, sweetie. Come in."

Suzanne, bursting with happiness and looking entrancing in flower-sprigged lilac, with miniature white and mauve orchids artfully tucked into her chestnut curls, burst into the room, hand in hand with Christine's niece, Fiona. Fiona looked lovely too, in her pink-tinged cream silk bridesmaid's gown, cream roses catching back the abundant blonde hair so like her mother's.

The two girls stood there and stared at Christine as though she looked at least a billion dollars.

Their gazes held love, approval, admiration. Heart melting, Christine circled slowly, inviting their inspection. She was wearing something from her own wardrobe. No one had seen it. It was an original; a famous couturier had actually fitted it on her. It was made of whisper-fine gold lace over silk, embroidered with sapphire-blue beads and crystals. In her hair, worn full and loose, was a single ornament—a sapphire flower, its gold stamens quivering with crystals. On her feet she wore high-heeled gold brocade pumps. In an effort not to eclipse anyone in the bridal party—certainly she couldn't overshadow the beautiful bride—she had elected to come just as "family".

"Oh, Chrissy, you look gorgeous! Absolutely great!" a glowing Suzanne said enthusiastically. She came to Christine and hugged her carefully, so as not to muss her. "You are so beautiful. Why can't I look like you?"

"Why would you need to, sweetheart?" Christine scoffed, encircling Suzanne with her arm. "You have a lovely look of your own. That dress is just perfect."

"Why wouldn't it be?" Suzanne responded with a flush of pleasure. "You chose it. And doesn't Fiona look wonderful?"

"She does indeed!" Christine held out her other arm. Kyall's beloved daughter, her niece Fiona, was so much like her mother, Sarah, it would have been laughable—only it was so heart-stopping it brought tears to Christine's eyes.

"Thank you, Chris. Thank you." Fiona's velvet-brown eyes were shimmery as she looked up at her new-found aunt. "Thank you everybody!"

High with excitement, she broke away and began to waltz around the room, before sinking into a deep curtsy that earned her Suzanne's and Christine's applause. Much to everyone's delight the cousins had bonded at first sight, eager to have one another's friendship and support. It was a state of affairs that was destined to be a great comfort and support throughout their lives.

"There are hundreds of people outside," Suzanne announced, running to the French doors and looking out at the beautiful sun-kissed scene.

"Isn't it the most wonderful thing I'm part of it all? Like a miracle!" Fiona looked overwhelmingly happy. "One day," she said solemnly, "I might write a book about it."

"I'm sure you will," Christine predicted. "You know you've inherited all your mother's beauty. In fact both of you have grown into stunning young ladies. Now, I suppose we'd better go out and join the party."

"Just wait until Mitch sees you!" Suzanne's face grew rosy with excitement. "Everyone will be turning to stare at you."

"Everyone will be too busy staring at the bride."

"We've seen her. She looks like an angel!" both girls said together.

"Mother is so happy she's glowing," Fiona said emotionally. "I have to say I'm a bit nervous."

Christine squeezed her hand. "You're going to be just fine," she promised, letting her love shine.

"Everything's got to be perfect."

"Oh, I'm so glad you came to us, Fee!" Suzanne's happiness was making her bloom like a rosebud opening under the warm sun. "I didn't know how beautiful life could be."

Hours later bride and groom stood on the verandah, facing their multitude of guests. They looked out on a sea of smiling faces, everyone sharing in the great joy. Shortly they were to fly away on the first leg of their honeymoon, but now seemed like a very good time to throw the bridal bouquet.

The bridesmaids were laughing, playfully enjoying themselves, gently jostling one another, and Christine was standing off a little to the left, with Mitch at her shoulder. Mitch, resplendent in his beautifully cut wedding suit, had been Kyall's best man. She was so full of bubbles, caused by happiness as much as the French champagne that had hit her bloodstream, and was so busy smiling meltingly at her fiancé, Mitch, she was unprepared as Sarah's exquisite bouquet soared towards her.

"You'd better catch that, Chrissy," Mitch urged, his

voice full of love and pride and a certain challenge. "This one has been a long time coming, but it's definitely for you!"

"How true!" She laughed in triumph, her long arm shooting up as the bouquet drifted on the buoyant air.

One of the wedding guests, with her eye on one of the Saunders brothers, made a valiant effort to catch it. But it sailed over her head as though it had a pre-ordained destination.

It landed in Christine's outstretched hand.

"Me!" she cried, her voice sparkling with elation.

Everyone started to clap. It was fantastic! She turned to look at Mitch, her face radiant over the top of the bouquet of fragrant flowers, reading his unswerving love in the brilliant sea-blue eyes.

"Congratulations, my love," he whooped, causing everyone to beam at them as though they'd helped plan where the bride's bouquet would land.

This was the greatest day Koomera Crossing had experienced in ages. Kyall McQueen and his beautiful Sarah were at long last married, rejoicing in their beautiful daughter who had been taken from them and miraculously returned.

And finally, after another interrupted relationship, the tremendously popular Mitch Claydon and their own homegrown celebrity Christine Reardon were back together again. It left the closely knit Outback town with a good feeling. A feeling that their great pioneering families stood united. They were an inspiration beyond dreams.

Weddings were perfect for bringing harmony.

* * * * *

Read over for a preview of
Shelley's story.
Coming soon in
Koomera Crossing
by Margaret Way

CHAPTER ONE

EXCITEMENT welled up so fast it made her dizzy. Brock Tyson. He stood there in the flesh. All fiery male pride. So much for the handsome daredevil boy. As a full-grown man he was magnificent, though the dark brooding hadn't died in him. She could see it as she faced him. The town, indeed the entire Outback, hadn't seen or heard of him in years but he was one of their own.

Daniel Brockway Tyson had been one of the wildest and certainly the most daring young men Koomera Crossing and the vast outlying station area had ever known. Brock had found all sorts of marvelous ways of living on the wild side. Sometimes, as a boy, he had gone off into the desert for days, giving no account of his adventures when he finally got home to Mulgaree. There had awaited him the predictable whipping. Mulgaree was the flagship of the Kingsley chain of cattle stations. Old Man Kingsley, Brock's grandfather, had run it like a private fiefdom. It was he who had done the whipping, but he'd never broken Brock's spirit.

"Why, if it isn't sweet little Shelley Logan," he drawled, a glimmer of genuine affection sparking his eyes. "How are you, darlin'?"

She'd been just a kid when he'd left, but already worth noticing. The enchanting little Logan twins. He hadn't forgotten the tragedy. There wouldn't be a soul for thousands of miles around who wasn't familiar with the sad story of how little Sean Logan had lost his life.

Shelley stared up into the face she'd once thought the

most beautiful in the world. Outside her twin. Probably she'd think that to the end of her life.

"Brock Tyson, you dangerous creature, that hurt!" She was breathless with shock and delight, her heart-shaped face radiant. "Where in the world did you spring from? I've been in town all day, yet not a single soul mentioned you were back—let alone right here in town."

An offer you can't afford to refuse!

High-valued coupons for upcoming books

A sneak peek at Harlequin's newest line—Harlequin Flipside™

Send away for a hardcover by *New York Times* bestselling author Debbie Macomber

How can you get all this?

Buy four Harlequin or Silhouette books during October–December 2003, fill out the form below and send the form and four proofs of purchase (cash register receipts) to the address below.

I accept this amazing offer!
Send me a coupon booklet:

Name (PLEASE PRINT)

Address   Apt. #

City   State/Prov.   Zip/Postal Code
                                                 098 KIN DXHT

Please send this form, along with your cash register receipts
as proofs of purchase, to:

In the U.S.:
Harlequin Coupon Booklet Offer, P.O. Box 9071, Buffalo, NY 14269-9071

In Canada:
Harlequin Coupon Booklet Offer, P.O. Box 609, Fort Erie, Ontario L2A 5X3

Allow 4–6 weeks for delivery. Offer expires December 31, 2003.
Offer good only while quantities last.

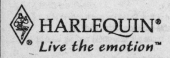

HARLEQUIN®
Live the emotion™

Silhouette®
Where love comes alive™

Visit us at www.eHarlequin.com

Q42003

If you enjoyed what you just read,
then we've got an offer you can't resist!

Take 2 bestselling love stories FREE!

Plus get a FREE surprise gift!

Your opinion is important to us! Please take a few moments to share your thoughts with us about your experiences with Harlequin and Silhouette books. Your comments will be very useful in ensuring that we deliver books you love to read. *Please take a few minutes to complete the questionnaire, then send it to us at the address below.*

Send your completed questionnaires to:
Harlequin/Silhouette Reader Survey, P.O. Box 9046, Buffalo, NY 14269-9046

---

1. As you may know, there are many different lines under the Harlequin and Silhouette brands. Each of the lines is listed below. Please check the box that most represents your reading habit for each line.

Line	Currently read this line	Do not read this line	Not sure if I read this line
Harlequin American Romance	❑	❑	❑
Harlequin Duets	❑	❑	❑
Harlequin Romance	❑	❑	❑
Harlequin Historicals	❑	❑	❑
Harlequin Superromance	❑	❑	❑
Harlequin Intrigue	❑	❑	❑
Harlequin Presents	❑	❑	❑
Harlequin Temptation	❑	❑	❑
Harlequin Blaze	❑	❑	❑
Silhouette Special Edition	❑	❑	❑
Silhouette Romance	❑	❑	❑
Silhouette Intimate Moments	❑	❑	❑
Silhouette Desire	❑	❑	❑

2. Which of the following best describes why you bought *this book?* One answer only, please.

the picture on the cover	❑	the title	❑
the author	❑	the line is one I read often	❑
part of a miniseries	❑	saw an ad in another book	❑
saw an ad in a magazine/newsletter	❑	a friend told me about it	❑
I borrowed/was given this book	❑	other: _____	❑

3. Where did you buy *this book?* One answer only, please.

at Barnes & Noble	❑	at a grocery store	❑
at Waldenbooks	❑	at a drugstore	❑
at Borders	❑	on eHarlequin.com Web site	❑
at another bookstore	❑	from another Web site	❑
at Wal-Mart	❑	Harlequin/Silhouette Reader	❑
at Target	❑	Service/through the mail	
at Kmart	❑	used books from anywhere	❑
at another department store or mass merchandiser	❑	I borrowed/was given this book	❑

4. On average, how many Harlequin and Silhouette books do you buy at one time?

I buy _____ books at one time	❑
I rarely buy a book	❑

MRQ403HR-1A

5. How many times per month do you shop for any *Harlequin and/or Silhouette* books?
One answer only, please.

1 or more times a week	❑	a few times per year	❑
1 to 3 times per month	❑	less often than once a year	❑
1 to 2 times every 3 months	❑	never	❑

6. When you think of your ideal heroine, which *one* statement describes her the best?
One answer only, please.

She's a woman who is strong-willed	❑	She's a desirable woman	❑
She's a woman who is needed by others	❑	She's a powerful woman	❑
She's a woman who is taken care of	❑	She's a passionate woman	❑
She's an adventurous woman	❑	She's a sensitive woman	❑

7. The following statements describe types or genres of books that you may be
interested in reading. Pick *up to 2 types* of books that you are most interested in.

I like to read about truly romantic relationships ❑
I like to read stories that are sexy romances ❑
I like to read romantic comedies ❑
I like to read a romantic mystery/suspense ❑
I like to read about romantic adventures ❑
I like to read romance stories that involve family ❑
I like to read about a romance in times or places that I have never seen ❑
Other: _____ ❑

*The following questions help us to group your answers with those readers who are
similar to you. Your answers will remain confidential.*

8. Please record your year of birth below.
19 ____

9. What is your marital status?
single ❑   married ❑   common-law ❑   widowed ❑
divorced/separated ❑

10. Do you have children 18 years of age or younger currently living at home?
yes ❑   no ❑

11. Which of the following best describes your employment status?
employed full-time or part-time ❑   homemaker ❑   student ❑
retired ❑   unemployed ❑

12. Do you have access to the Internet from either home or work?
yes ❑   no ❑

13. Have you ever visited eHarlequin.com?
yes ❑   no ❑

14. What state do you live in?
_____

15. Are you a member of Harlequin/Silhouette Reader Service?
yes ❑   Account # _____   no ❑   MRQ403HR-1B

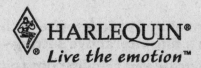